NOT TO GLORIFY BUT
SITUATIONS IN THE H

JIM AND JACKE

Hello, my name is Larry W. Keys

I have written a Hoodzville Step Musical called, JIM and JACKEE. Where I take the NEGATIVE emotions and turn it INTO the POSITIVE attributes of my street characters.

With this step musical, I promote the Goal of building on the strengths of each individual character to become a ROLE MODEL. I create a supportive environment negative and positive, in order to fit the therapeutic approach to the needs of each individual in their playground and school.

I Identify key attachment needs for them to heal from their traumatic experiences. Then I use a direct response of – Joy – Sadness (hurt) – Fear and Shame to bring forth an idea that enlightens them to realize their situation.

By doing this, their Unmet Attachment Needs of Love, Connection, and Security are

NOT TO GLORIFY BUT, ONLY TO IDENTIFY THOSE SITUATIONS IN THE HOODZ.

met through positive thinking. The Problem-Solving and Consolidation of those attachment needs, have led to promoting the acceptance of my character's experience.

This encouraged my characters to be in touch with the part inside of them, that is an "antidote" to the negative perceptions. In the end, this will lead them to a SERIOUS HOODZVILLE STEP MUSICAL along with 8 songs. My script identifies with hard to reach kids who may need Role Models in their life.

Hopes and encouragement for our young, and soon to be adults.

Sincerely
Larry W. Keys
Larrywkeys.com

NOT TO GLORIFY BUT, ONLY TO IDENTIFY THOSE
SITUATIONS IN THE HOODZ.

INTRO: COUNTRY'S HOME – THAT

MORNING

(SONG – DRIVE BYS)

(Young gangsters Jim, Country and Lander at
Lander's mother house, down the bottom of the
hood in South Hoodzville. Make their plans to
scoop some drugs to use and sell.)

COUNTRY and JIM laughed at LANDER
while he was looking like a big time Gangster.
But then it was JIM'S turn to play gangster and
he lift up his sweatshirt and showed his rod to
Country so he would know for sure that they
meant business.

They all burst out laughing this time because
they were still Yangsters in route to becoming
GANGSTERS. (So they thought)

JIM said, "And hurry up man I'm ill!"

NOT TO GLORIFY BUT, ONLY TO IDENTIFY THOSE SITUATIONS IN THE HOODZ.

Country grinned and said.

COUNTRY "No problem, I got the easy part, see you in a few."

As they walked Country down the steps out the front door.

LANDER'S MOTHER "Close my door boy, cause you letting out my heat!"

His mother shouted from in the kitchen as she approached the living room where they were.

Then Jim and Lander shut the door, as they headed for the stairs to Lander's room. Lander's mother just happens to peep out the window because she saw flashing lights through her curtains and she said.

LANDER'S MOTHER "I wonder what Country did, I don't understand it, and he is such a nice kid."

NOT TO GLORIFY BUT, ONLY TO IDENTIFY THOSE
SITUATIONS IN THE HOODZ.

Then she turned to Lander and Jim as they
stopped halfway up the stairs and said.

LANDER'S MOTHER "I don't know what
he did but, you'd bet not be involved Lander!"

LANDER "We don't know nothing, mom!"

Lander was looking all pitiful about the
situation then they both went upstairs to
Landers window and watched the police
handcuff Country.

Jim asked Lander with a puzzling look on his
face.

JIM "I wonder why they snatched him up."

Jim and Country both were light skinned, slim,
with short afros.

Jim looked at Lander.

JIM "Maybe he looks like me."

NOT TO GLORIFY BUT, ONLY TO IDENTIFY THOSE SITUATIONS IN THE HOODZ.

LANDER "Got dam, you right come to think of it."

Then Jim, as he holds back some tears, said.

JIM "I don't think he's going to do the time for me?"

Jim sat down beside Lander, not only ill from not shootin some dope, but also scared to death. The cold steel was against his thigh only to remind him of what he had done earlier.

This stuff was serious enough for him to rock back and forth and almost pray. Ill from not havin dope in his system (body), and scared that Country was going to snitch on him about the money.

Jim was reluctant to look out the window again. But his curiosity got the best of him, all of a sudden Jim looked out the window again and Country was being put into the police car. Country looked up at Lander and Jim in the window with a terrifying look of fear.

NOT TO GLORIFY BUT, ONLY TO IDENTIFY THOSE
SITUATIONS IN THE HOODZ.

**Seem like Country and Jim felt the same fear.
Jim left Lander's house, went around the back
way up the street to his home. When Jim
entered the house he smelled refer (marijuana)
and asked his mom what that smell was.**

**As usual she denied any smell as she tried to fan
away the smoke talkin bout a fly was in the
house. Jim did a half smile then went to his
room and sat down on the side of his bed and
thought of how his life started out. He didn't
start out a bad kid, OR DID HE?**

**He thought about his brother Mickey and years
gone by; Mickey was locked up again as usual
for fighting. Then Jim eyes begin to get heavy
from all the excitement, he closed one eye to
think about what had just happened that day.**

**He drifted into a nod as his thoughts begin to
come together. (Still thinking, one eye was half
open the other closed) He thought about how he
hung out with the guys who stole cars, ate pills,
shot dope, and the excitement of selling dope.**

NOT TO GLORIFY BUT, ONLY TO IDENTIFY THOSE
SITUATIONS IN THE HOODZ.

Then he thought to himself, (maybe I'm
addicted to selling dope?) but from all this he
was beginning to become a problem. The
problem child he said that he wouldn't be
because of his brother.

Now the only thing he dwelled on was keeping
his parents off his back so he could continue the
stuff that he was doing. With his mom and dad
caught up in the drug world now, (smoking
weed) it became harder for him to fool them
about what he was doing.

So, school was his only way to keep them off his
case. Then his mind flashed back to his
situation, he thought to himself while looking
out the window. (Where did I go wrong? Now
somebody who looks like me is going to jail. OR
WAS HE?)

Jim said out loud.

   JIM "Country bet not snitch on me!"

NOT TO GLORIFY BUT, ONLY TO IDENTIFY THOSE
SITUATIONS IN THE HOODZ.

As he wiped a tear from his eye, he grabbed his
stomach, then wiped his nose, and rolled across
the bed in pain. Then another thought came to
him.

(If only I had some dope, I could work this mess
out!)

Jim rolled off the bed and headed for the door,
as he slammed the door shut with a nasty
attitude he thought out loud with strong
feelings.

JIM "I'M GONNA GET ME SOME DAM
DOPE TODAY!!!!

As Jim walked down the steps of the apartment
he lived in, the door swung open with Mark and
his girl swinging on his arm. She lived
downstairs from Jim.

MARK "Hey Jim, your boy Hectors brother
is throwing down at the Med. Center man, he
be getting paid with that weed."

NOT TO GLORIFY BUT, ONLY TO IDENTIFY THOSE
SITUATIONS IN THE HOODZ.

Jim answered him with a puzzling look on his
face.

   JIM "Weed don't sell that great around
here, and you know it!"

Jim starting to feel weak from not eating and no
dope, Mark said as they walked by him.

   MARK "It sells like crazy when you lace it
with cocaine. Man he be selling $2 joints and
getting paid!"

   JIM "Oh he is, is he?"

In a sly voice.

Then he knew how he was going to get his blast.
He checked his dip, positioned his rodscoe for
easy access to pull out, cocked his hat further to
the side, and headed for the Med. Center.

The Med. Center was up the street around the
backside of the school yard. When Jim got there
he stood by a tree and watched the junkies line

up for those joints, Jim pulled out his rod and
said to himself;

JIM "He lucky I don't do no cocaine!"

As he approached Ronnie he noticed a woman
next in line as he got closer the woman looked
familiar to him. Then he saw that it was his
mother, he quickly made a B-line (detour)
through the crowd.

Then he walked around the school to the
playground on the other side, mad as hell. Now
his mom is on that stuff, tears came to his eyes
and he cried out loud.

JIM "Lord, wha-chu doin to me? I can't take
this no-more!"

As Jim continued to the playground his face
was filled with tears. As soon as he stepped on
the playground he fell to his knees. took out his
rod and start digging a hole with it.

Not knowing who was there he continued to talk

to himself, about himself, asking for the lord to have mercy on him because he didn't mean to turn out this way.

The deeper he dug in the ground the harder he cried. Finally, he stopped, threw the gun in the hole stood up and starts kicking the dirt back in the hole. Then, the girl Jackee, from his school who was about his age was there.

She didn't take any stuff from nobody, she was there with her little brother and sister to play safely in the playground. So, she was the one picking up wine bottles, jar tops with left over drugs in them, along with glue bags and needles.

She walked over to Jim with this brown paper bag filled with drug stuff and looked over at Jim as he stood there with a long face.

JACKEE "You finish yet? Cause I like to clean up and you in my way!"

Jim looked at her as she bent down by his feet

and picked up another needle and put it in the bag.

JIM "You mean to tell me that you clean this whole playground up by yourself?"

Jackee looked over at her brother and sister and then looked at Jim and said.

JACKEE "When they get old enough they'll help out too, so other kids after them can have a safe place to play."

Jim wiped his face and said.

JIM "Then I guess I better take my rod from outta that hole huh?"

Jackee said with an attitude.

JACKEE "If you're throwin it away then let's bury it deeper than that!"

Jim smiled a little and said.

NOT TO GLORIFY BUT, ONLY TO IDENTIFY THOSE
SITUATIONS IN THE HOODZ.

JIM "Yeah you right, I need to go a little
deeper or one of those future kids you talkin
bout will dig it up."

Then Jim looked over at her little brother and
sister, when he looked back at her she was
walking toward the guy named Mac, who had
just entered the playground.

JACKEE "Oh no, the playground is closed
big boy! No more junkies this morning."

MAC "Who in the hell you talkin too girl,
I'll kick your ass!"

Jackee stepped back and stooped down by the
fence never taking her eyes off of Mac, and
stood back up with a long 2x4 stick and said.

JACKEE "You gonna do what?"

Just then Jim walked over to Mac and said.

JIM "You heard her, go somewhere else!"

As he balled up his fist, he stood between Mac
and Jackee facing Mac. Mac looked at Jim and
said.

MAC "Look little Mickey, I ain't got no beef
wit-chu.
She can't be keeping us out of here during the
daytime who do she think she is? I need to sit
down and get my blast!"

Jim raised his fist and said.

JIM "There ain't no more us junkie, I quit!"

Then he punched Mac square in his right eye.
Mac put up his dukes (guards/hands) and
Jackee swung the 2x4 stick and it cracked
across Mac's shoulder then he screamed out
loud.

MAC "Oh, shucks!"

Then took he off running. Jackee's brother and
sister were so busy playing that they didn't

notice the trouble. Jim looked at Jackee and
Jackee looked at Jim. She put her stick back
down next to the fence and Jim walked over to
the hole where the rod was buried.

Starts digging a deeper hole for his, use-to-be
rodscoe. Jackee looked over at Jim and said.

JACKEE "Are you serious about no more
drugs?"

Jim looked up at her with his eyes open wide
and a big smile then said.

JIM "I don't need it anymore."

Jackee reached out her hand and Jim reached
out his hand and they shook hands. Then
Jackee got on her knees to help him bury the
rodscoe. They both looked up and saw two
more little kids come to the playground.

Jackee's little brother and sister ran over to
greet them playing a game of tag. Jackee looked
at Jim and said.

NOT TO GLORIFY BUT, ONLY TO IDENTIFY THOSE
SITUATIONS IN THE HOODZ.

JACKEE "I told you!"

Jim just smiled and said.

JIM "I see, you were right."

They stood up and start collecting the junkie's
mess, and then Jackee said.

JACKEE "If you want I'll help you kick your
habit; only if you want me too."

As she battered her eyes up and down and
kicked some more dirt over the hole.

Jim said with a smile once again.

JIM "Ok, cause I think I'm gonna need some
help to go cold turkey." (Straight sober)

Jackee smiled and then Jim smiled back.

JACKEE "I think I'm gonna need some help
too, cleaning up is a big job for a little girl like
me."

The whole time looking into Jim's eyes and smiling, then Jim looked at Jackee and said.

JIM "Pass me that junk bag, girl!"

Jackee passed Jim the junk bag and headed toward the other side of the playground with such a serious look. As she walked away she mumbled something with a smirk look on her face.

JACKEE "Here we go again!"

She said to herself. Jim looked pass her and at the other side of the playground was Kathy; they call her Cat for short. Because the girl could fight so well and she would scratch you up like a cat. She was a mean junky.

As Jackee walked past the kids (her brother and sister and their friends) she waved for them to go down there where Jim was standing.

Mikee said sarcastically.

NOT TO GLORIFY BUT, ONLY TO IDENTIFY THOSE SITUATIONS IN THE HOODZ.

MIKEE "For what, it ain't like he gonna tell us a story or something, Jackee!"

As he was being chased by another kid he headed toward the other end of the playground after he saw Jackee's look that she had on her face. Then they all migrated down to that end of the playground where Jim was standing.

He looks on as Jackee and cat were battling with words then the body language let Jim know that they were about to get it on. CeCe, Mikee, Joey, and other little kids stood there with Jim and CeCe said.

CECE "Now we can watch them fight or you gonna tell us a story?"

They all begin to laugh at Jim, but, Jim was more concern about Jackee. He never use to care about people before he hooked up with Jackee, even as just a friend.

Then Jim saw Cat reach out with her hands and

NOT TO GLORIFY BUT, ONLY TO IDENTIFY THOSE
SITUATIONS IN THE HOODZ.

Jackee put up her hands to protect her face.
Jim took one step toward the other side of the
playground and Mikee and Joey stepped in
front of him and Mikee said.

MIKEE "So whaz it gonna be JUNKY, a
story or a fight?"

Jim looked down at them kids and instead of
four of them he counted seven, then Jim Said.

JIM "Hold up shawty, I'm here to help, I'm
on your side. You couldn't handle my stories,
cause you have to think too hard to figure them
out!"

JOEY "Oh yeah, try us!"

MIKEE "Yeah, come on with it, SHAWTY!"

Then they all laughed at Jim for a second or
two. As Jim begins his story he watches as
Jackee hit Cat in the face then he thought to
himself, (Dam, Jackee fights just like a boy).

Then all of a sudden Cat charged Jackee and
Jackee put up her hands again to protect her
face, then stepped to one side and kicked Cat
straight in the stomach. Cat bent over
screaming and out of breath gagging.

Then Jackee hit her once then twice and that's
all he needed to see and he began his story with.

   JIM "God bless the fools and babes, the
simple minded jack of all trades. Once upon a
time there was this bum and he was his
mother's only son. He wore one shoe on one
shoe off his feet, looking in trash cans for
something to eat."

Jim looked over to where Jackee and Cat were,
only to see Cat running out of the playground
fast as possible.

As Jim smiled he continued his story as he
watches CeCe put her hand over her mouth to
cover up her sleepy yarn, and Mikee making a
snoring sound.

NOT TO GLORIFY BUT, ONLY TO IDENTIFY THOSE SITUATIONS IN THE HOODZ.

(JIM BEGINS STORY #1)

JIM "Three guys, one stopped to talk to the bum as the other guys just watch and laugh as he waits for his buddy."

#1 KID "whaz-up man? Remember me man, remember the time your grandma whips your butt for trippin me at the playground when we were kids?"

BUM "Nope, I remember she told me about this battlefield that's out here."

As he tried to go around the guy the other guy stepped in his way.

#1 KID "Man, I still got the scar from that day when we all played in the playground. We played putting in the box and you cheated by trippin me cause you couldn't catch me, remember?"

BUM "Nope! I caught hell about this

battlefield out here from grandma! She called me in the house and opened the curtains and pointed out there and said, "You're on the battlefield!"

#2 KID "Then why you come back outside cryin like you got your butt beat?"

Bum "Cause my grandma scared me about this battlefield we're on."
#1 kid "You mean to tell me, after all these years, you just getting around to tellin me this!"

BUM "Nobody asked me, you all just teased me cause I was cryin."

#3 KID "What battlefield your grandma told chu bout? Man, she must have been seeing things."

As they both laughed.

BUM "She said, we're on the battlefield for the LORD, and that I was in GOD's army."

NOT TO GLORIFY BUT, ONLY TO IDENTIFY THOSE SITUATIONS IN THE HOODZ.

#1KID "Come on Man, thaz all she said and you cried like a little baby, no wonder we teased you!"

BUM "She said she was on the battlefield too. It wasn't what she said it was how she said it that scared me. When I came to tell ya'll what she said you all just kept on teasin me about a butt whippin."

#1 KID "Man, I'm ready for any battle that comes along, I got connections for any type of gun. Thaz how long you been gone, I'm the man now!"

BUM "I use to think that before I left to go to war, now I see and feel the battlefield every day."

#2 KID "Man, you crazy, shell shocked and all that!"

Walking away.

#3 KID "Come on Man, let's go." Bum said,

NOT TO GLORIFY BUT, ONLY TO IDENTIFY THOSE SITUATIONS IN THE HOODZ.

"Here's my weapon!"

Secretly showing him the bible under his coat.

BUM "And I rebuke you in the name of JESUS! And he shall flee from thee!"

(Pointing at the guys as they walked away laughing at him)

(MEANWHILE)

Jim looked down at the kids as they were beginning to sit down on the seesaw and some leaning on the fence.

JIM "Ok, now that's your story, now go play!"

MIKEE "What happen to the bum?"

CECE "He musta died and went to heaven."

JOEY "Naw man, don't leave us hanging!"

NOT TO GLORIFY BUT, ONLY TO IDENTIFY THOSE
SITUATIONS IN THE HOODZ.

Jackee came over their sweating and fixing her
knit hat back over her hair tucking the hair
under the hat. You see, she was a pretty light
brown skin slim girl with long brown hair.

Jackee said with a smile.

JACKEE "Yeah Jim, don't leave us
hanging."

JIM "Ok this is it, ya'll go play after this
one."

CECE "Are they big kids or little kids?"

JOEY "Big kids stupid!"

Mikee said in a stern voice

MIKEE "Alright Joey, watch it!"

Joey looked at Mikee as he balled up his fist
looking at his sister CeCe's sad face for calling
her stupid, then Joey realized he had hurt
CeCe's feelings. Joey put his arm around CeCe

26

shoulder and said.

JOEY "CeCe you know I was just playin girl."

CeCe smiled while looking at Jim and said.

CECE "Ok, let's hear the story, Jim the story teller."

Everybody laughed even Jim and Jackee. Then Jim start looking all serious and stuff as he thought more into his story, then he said.

JIM "Ok, but you have to think real hard because the bum is very important to this story."

(THEN JIM BEGIN STORY #2)

As two guys walked down the street they walk by the bum look him up and down and then decide to tease him by not letting him get by either side of them.

NOT TO GLORIFY BUT, ONLY TO IDENTIFY THOSE
SITUATIONS IN THE HOODZ.

#1 KID "Hey man, I heard you use to be
good with your hands, back in the day. Also
that you use to have a vicious (nasty) left hook."

Bum look at him seriously and said.

BUM "I heard her scream, did you hear
her?"

#2 KID "Hey man, they say when you came
back from the war you weren't right in the
head, whaz up with that?"

The Bum said as he spaced out looking beyond
them.

BUM "Don't forget what my older brother
told-cha!"

#1 kid said as he looked at his buddy with a
surprised look.

#1 KID "Man, they say you're an only child,
you ain't got no older brother!"

NOT TO GLORIFY BUT, ONLY TO IDENTIFY THOSE SITUATIONS IN THE HOODZ.

Then, they both laughed.

The bum looked at the #1 kid and said.

BUM "She hollered, BLOODY MURDA!"

#1 KID "Man, I art to bust a cap in your butt talkin bout murda!"

Then the bum said.

BUM "I was only 8 and he was just 11, he told me that; some don't get to heaven!"

As he opened his coat to show his bible.

#2 Kid grabbed his buddy by the arm and said.

#2 KID "Man, you lucky we got to go, or I'd bust a cap in you myself. Then again; who you lookin at?"

As the bum jump back he takes one step to the side of the kids and shouts with his coat wide open and chest stuck out showing his bible.

BUM "I rebuke you in the name of JESUS! And they shall flee from thee!"

Just then a car rolls by and shots are fired, the 2 guys take off running up the street and a lady screams.

LADY "MURDA! MURDA!"

One kid screams back.

#1 KID "I'm gonna kick your butt when I see you again!"

As he run down the street with his gun in his hand ducking trying to avoid getting hit by bullets. Then the Bum said.

BUM "I heard her scream bloody murda. That's when I learned how to pray."

Then the bum reaches inside his coat and pulls out his bible and waves it in the air and shouts.

BUM "There's only one, who can't be beat!"

They all begin to clap after that story and Jackee was impressed with Jim keeping their attention.

Then CeCe waved two girls to come over as they were walking in the playground on their way to go jump rope. CeCe shouted to the girls.

CECE "its story tellin time."

Jim was on a roll and smiled at the applause he had gotten just now. Jim said.

JIM "Ok, ok, this is it no more after this and I mean it!"

Jim looked hard at Mikee and Joey and pointed at CeCe for acknowledgement. She shook her head up and down, and then Jackee snapped to attention and saluted Jim. Making everybody laugh when she said.

NOT TO GLORIFY BUT, ONLY TO IDENTIFY THOSE
SITUATIONS IN THE HOODZ.

JACKEE "Yes sir, and thank you sir!"

Jim was beginning to feel a little rough from not
getting a blast but it seems to go away as he
found something to laugh about, and that was
Jackee and her crew. Then Jim began for the
last time for that day.

(Story #3)

(SONG – ONE 2-MANY)

JIM as a Junky high on drugs walked up to
the bum the junky asked, Hey man, how can I
get off this stuff man, cause its killin me?
Hmmm, Hmmm."

Then he reaches out for a handshake or high
five. The Bum said in a stern voice and serious
face.

BUM "One is too many, and a thousand not
enough, we ain't playin, we ain't taken no
stuff!"

NOT TO GLORIFY BUT, ONLY TO IDENTIFY THOSE
SITUATIONS IN THE HOODZ.

Then the Junky said,

JUNKY "Come on man, they say you went to
rehab after you came home from the war. Look
at you, now you don't use drugs any more.
Hmmm, Hmmm."

Then the bum said

BUM "I got there just before it was too late."

JUNKY "Man, I think if you can kick a drug
habit then so can I. Hmmm, hmmm, wha-chu
think?"

As the junky leaned over to shake the bum
hand the bum sat down on the street curb and
then the junky sat down also.

BUM "I'll tell you a story of his goodness
and his glory."

JUNKY "Ok man, this better be good, cause
I got places to go and people to see."

NOT TO GLORIFY BUT, ONLY TO IDENTIFY THOSE SITUATIONS IN THE HOODZ.

As he leaned forward to listen with his eyes closed like he was falling asleep.

BUM "There were these 3 kids that were in a shelter for trouble kids on the corner of 4th and 5th street.

#1 KID "I got transferred here just so I could take you out, chump! Bust you up!"

#2 KID "Think you bad huh? You never could do it out there, what makes you think you can do it here at this young training school they call a shelter, huh?"

#1 KID "Your posse, your click, you ain't got nobody to back you up now!"

(looking around)

#2 KID "I got somebody to watch my back! It's GOD, and we don't play that!"

#1KID "Who dat, who dat? Tell me who G-O-D is?"

NOT TO GLORIFY BUT, ONLY TO IDENTIFY THOSE
SITUATIONS IN THE HOODZ.

A third kid come walking by them.

THIRD KID "Beam me up SCOTTIE, hey,
hey, hey, beam me up SCOTTIE before I go to
pray!"

#1 KID "Keep walkin Simp, before I bust
you up too!"

#2 KID "You don't want to touch him, he got
me started, told me about the red sea and how it
got parted."

#1 Kid said with a puzzling look on his face.

1 KID "Man, what you talkin bout. GOD,
red sea, ya'll can't do nothing with me!"

#3 kid stopped and looked at them and said.

3 KID "I know you 'all not gonna fight, I
remember when we all use to be tight. In school,
after school, but that was so long ago, hey kid
wha-chu know?"

NOT TO GLORIFY BUT, ONLY TO IDENTIFY THOSE SITUATIONS IN THE HOODZ.

#1 KID "Keep steppin before I tear your head off!"

#2 KID "He can't help himself, now mess with me and see wha-chu get!"

Then #3 kid stepped beside #2 kid and said.

#3 KID "Cause if it ain't ruff, it ain't us, now who you rollin whit?"

Then the #1 kid backed up and said.

1 "Man you always got somebody watchin you back!"

As he started to walk away #2 kid said.

2 KID "Man, what he do for me he can do for you. He knows what we go thru."

#1 KID "now who you talkin bout, GOD, or Simp-Jack Baby!"

#2 KID "Now chill out man and have a good day, cause me and Simp-jack goin over there to pray."

And he pointed to a sign on the wall that read, JESUS SAVES, and an arrow pointed with words over top of it that read, THIS WAY TO PRAY.

(BACK TO THE JUNKY AND BUM)

JUNKY "So did they go pray or not, or did they jump him and whip his butt. Then again, what does this have to do with how you got sober man, hmmmm, hmmmm?"

Then the Bum said in his unusual riddles.

BUM "Strugglin and strivin, simpjack conniving. It took G-O-D and me to stop killin me! Now wha-chu think?"

JUNKY "Ok man, I told you I had some where to go, people to see and stuff to do."

As he got up and staggered on down the street
shaking his head and waving his hand at the
bum. The bum smiled and got up and reached
in his coat pulled out his bible and raised it to
the sky and said.

BUM "Forgive them father for they know
not what they do. Thank you Jesus!"

Then he waved back at the junky with his bible
in hand and said.

BUM "Have a bless day my brother."

Then Jim quickly said out loud.

JIM "THE END!"

Now being a ROLE MODEL gave him an
attitude of gratitude. The kids jumped up and
down start whistling, Jackee ran over to Jim
and hugged him, then they all rushed him at
once.

NOT TO GLORIFY BUT, ONLY TO IDENTIFY THOSE
SITUATIONS IN THE HOODZ.

It looked like a big group hug, but, by Jim not being use to that type of emotional uproar. All of a sudden tears of joy came from out of nowhere and Jackee wiped his tears with her shirt sleeve.

(ONE YEAR LATER)

One year went by, Jim's mother had died of an OD (over dose) and his father was locked up for murdering the drug dealer who sold her the drugs.

Jim stayed with relatives and friends and survived the times with a positive outlook on life. Jim and Jackee was a pair to be reckoned with when it came down to the safety of those kids in the playground.

Times were rough and they kept pressing on, not knowing where this act of faith of keeping this playground safe would lead them in the future. There was this one particular dope dealer (Percy) about their age that was very interested in the playground.

NOT TO GLORIFY BUT, ONLY TO IDENTIFY THOSE
SITUATIONS IN THE HOODZ.

Jim and Jackee had to stay on top of their game
in order to keep him out. Then Percy got bolder
and continuing to invade their playground after
hours late at night, and one day it happened.

(PLAYGROUND INVASION)

Across the street on the unlit side there were
three men with black sweatshirts on, trying to
look inconspicuous. On the back of their
sweatshirts in small white letters (police) is
written.

The young boy Percy on the other side of the
street has his boys move the shoeshine stand
closer toward the playground because he had a
strong feeling about those three guys across
from him.

As Percy lean over the shoe shine box two guys
walk up handed him some money. Then one guy
put his foot on the shoe shine box and one of
Percy boys kneel down, reached in the box, pull
out a rag and brush then wipe off the guy shoes.

Then as he shook his hand left a bag of dope in
the guy's hand. This is often repeated during
the shoeshine operation. Then a girl walks up,
and Percy and his crew do the same thing over
again.

As Percy moves closer to the playground Jim
and his crew, with Jackee and her crew both
looked around watching for junkies and dealers
trying to move in. If they let either one cut
through the playground their peace of mind
would be in jeopardy.

(MEANWHILE AT THE PLAYGROUND)

Jim and his crew were gathered around a table
playing chess and checkers while keeping an eye
out on the perimeter of the playground at the
same time. They were constantly checking each
other for contact fighting.

If one junkie or dealer step foot on the
playground there would be a loud whistle and
guys and girls would come running over to

where they were and usher them off (direct them) into another direction around the playground.

There were also little girls playing hopscotch and jump rope. Then Jackee walked over to Jim tapped him on the shoulder and said, "It's time." Jim waved to a couple of guys to follow him.

Jackee waved to a couple of girls and they gathered around at another table. This was the main event, the sign on the table read.

(THE TABLE OF CHAMPIONS)

Jim sat down and then Jackee sat down, both put one arm on the table the other behind their back. Somebody said;

  CROWD "On your mark, get set, ready, go!"

The crowd cheered as people hollered out;

NOT TO GLORIFY BUT, ONLY TO IDENTIFY THOSE
SITUATIONS IN THE HOODZ.

CROWD "go Jackee, go Jim."

Jim had Jackee's hand almost down then
Jackee came back, Jackee had Jim, then Jackee,
then Jim.

Suddenly "BAM" Jim's back of his hand
smacked the table and the crowd roared.
(Cheering Jackee on) Jim smiled as he got up
and winked his eye at Jackee. Then the next guy
sat down and the game started again.

As the crowd roared Jackee got up and then
somebody else sat down. As the crowd cheered
the other two people, two guys started playing a
beat on the bongo's and Congo drums.

Two girls walked over and picked two jump
ropes up and another started singing and
rapping to the beat. Jackee stood beside Jim as
they watched the arm wrestle event and then
they all started singing together.

GIRLS "On my block kids are sellin dope,
11, 12. and 13, some say their man hood would

never be seen, try to talk to them you look like
you're crazy, some you get through too and
some are plain lazy, etc. etc. etc."

As the singing went on Percy and his crew were
getting closer and closer with the police close
behind. When the junkies that scooped from
Percy tried to take a short cut through the
playground Jim and some guys, Jackee and
some girls stopped them.

(SONG - ON MY BLOCK)

Standing in front of them shaking their heads
no, and pointing for them to go around. Next
thing you know Percy and his crew was at the
playground trying to get through.

**(UNDER THE STREET LIGHTS IN FRONT
OF THE PLAYGROUND)**

Percy and his crew with Jim and his crew begin
to step to each other. Percy said as he sized Jim
up for battle.

NOT TO GLORIFY BUT, ONLY TO IDENTIFY THOSE
SITUATIONS IN THE HOODZ.

PERCY "I want that playground to sell my
drugs!"

Jim said as he kept coming forward.

JIM "this is our playground and you got
some nerve trying to get through!"

Then they step to each other's face and threw
up fists and the battle began. A right, then a
left, then another right, both guys were
matching each other blow for blow then all the
others begin to step forward and throw
punches. As soon as it started it stopped
because the police blew their whistles.

They came out from nowhere and began to
chase both crews. Among the few that were
caught were Percy and Jim. Although both
crews were together in the paddy wagon (police
cruiser), they still talked smack to each other.
They were separated after the cuffs came off of
them at Hoodzville South police station.

NOT TO GLORIFY BUT, ONLY TO IDENTIFY THOSE
SITUATIONS IN THE HOODZ.

(LATER THAT AFTERNOON)

Standing in front of the judge clean and dressed
up, Percy was asked by the judge.

JUDGE "How do he plea?"

Percy said in his best speaking voice.

PERCY "Well, your honor as you know, I
have a repredible business establishment as a
shoe shine stand. Being the oldest in my family
of three brothers and two sisters, I of course,
have to help my mother support the family. You
know like, my father ran off with my mother's
only sister, and took all of our money with
him."

The judge looked up from his papers with his
thick reading glasses that were hanging on to
the tip of his nose. They were just about to fall
off, if it weren't for the string tied around his
neck holding them on.

Judge asked in a stern voice.

NOT TO GLORIFY BUT, ONLY TO IDENTIFY THOSE
SITUATIONS IN THE HOODZ.

JUDGE "I asked you how do you plea!"

Percy looking all dumb founded answered.

PERCY "I plead not guilty, uh, you
hinniest."

Everyone laughed but the judge. The judge
looked over at the bailiff as he smiled and
whispered.

JUDGE "He almost had me fooled for a
minute."

Then smacked his hammer on the desk and
said.

JUDGE "Sixty days at Boys Village!"

Percy looked at Jim and balled his fist up
saying.

PERCY "I'm gonna get you for this!"

NOT TO GLORIFY BUT, ONLY TO IDENTIFY THOSE
SITUATIONS IN THE HOODZ.

Jim balled his fist up and said.

JIM "Come on, you feelin Froggy? Then
leap, chump!"

The judge smacked his hammer on the desk and
said.

JUDGE "Order in this court room, BAM,
BAM, order in this court room!"

As he pounded on his desk. Then the judge
leaned over to the bailiff and whispered.

JUDGE "Look at him, at least he could have
put on some descent clothes before he goes to
jail."

The bailiff and the judge chuckled a little. Then
the judge asked.

JUDGE "Young man how do you plea?"

Jim looked up at the judge and said.

NOT TO GLORIFY BUT, ONLY TO IDENTIFY THOSE SITUATIONS IN THE HOODZ.

JIM "Not guilty!"

The judge looked at the bailiff, smiled and said.

JUDGE "Thirty days at the youth shelter!"

Jim said in a loud with an attitude in his voice.

JIM "Wha-chu talkin bout judge, I didn't do nothin wrong!"

The judge leaned over to the bailiff and said.

JUDGE "Watch me shut him up."

Turned and looked at Jim and said.

JUDGE "Keep it up boy and I'll charge you five days for contempt!"

Then Jim stood up and said.

JIM "Who you callin Boy?"

The judge was leaning over giving the bailiff a

high five as Jim was saying this. Then he turned around and looked at Jim with cold eyes and smacked his hammer on his desk and said.

JUDGE "5 days for contempt!"

Jim shouted at the judge with anger.

JIM "I keep the peace where I come from, why I got to go to jail?"

JUDGE "Cause you got too much mouth!"

(BAM, BAM)

JUDGE "Five more days!"

Jim shouted once again.

JIM "Oh yeah, I wish it was you out there I was fightin!"

Something went BAM, BAM, BAM.

JUDGE "order in this courtroom!"

NOT TO GLORIFY BUT, ONLY TO IDENTIFY THOSE
SITUATIONS IN THE HOODZ.

The judge then pointed at Jim and shouted.

   JUDGE "Five more days!"

As the bailiff headed for Jim to cuff him, the
judge added five more days.
All the people in the court room from both
crews were laughing at this scene that the judge
was feeding into, by Jim facing off with the
judge. (Talking back) As the bailiff pulled Jim
out the courtroom Jim shouted.

   JIM "You should have seen those little kids
out there playin, you should have been there;
you old fart!"

The judge hammer went "BAM, BAM"

   JUDGE "that's five more days, keep
talking!"

Then the judge stood up and pointed at the
door and said.

NOT TO GLORIFY BUT, ONLY TO IDENTIFY THOSE
SITUATIONS IN THE HOODZ.

JUDGE "Get him out of here!"

The people in the court room stood up clapped
at this spectacle that was happening. Jackee,
JoJo, Mikee, CeCe, Saraj, Brenda, Kent, and
others went out the court room door laughing
as Jim was being taken away. The judge, while
still standing shouted once again.

JUDGE "Clear this court room, before I lock
all you fools up; get out, get out!"

So therefore Jim had to serve 20 days in a
holding cell at a training school facility before
he was transferred to the youth shelter.

(20 DAYS LATER AT THE SHELTER)

The secretary Miss Margie called from her
desk.

MARGIE "Jim, Jim, anyone out their name
Jim?"

Out of the 3 boys and one man, no one

answered. Then the secretary called out another
name, then 5 minutes later another name. One
by one each person stood up and walked up to
the big brown door, opened it and never came
back.

Finally, a lady came out of the office where the
brown door was and asked the secretary Miss
Margie if Jim ever showed up. Miss Brewster
was in charge of the shelter.

BREWSTER "Where is Jim Miss Margie?
Have you seen him yet? It's getting mighty
late."

MARGIE "No Miss Brewster, I haven't seen
him yet."

Then Miss Margie leaned over and asked Jim.

MARGIE "Your name isn't Jim is it?"

Jim answered with a smile.

JIM "Yes ma'am it is."

NOT TO GLORIFY BUT, ONLY TO IDENTIFY THOSE SITUATIONS IN THE HOODZ.

The secretary (lost it), she stood up and slammed one hand on her desk and pointed a finger with the other hand at Jim saying, (with every other word her finger pointing up and down at him).

MARGIE "I don't know what your problem is but, you better get it together because, we are here to help you, not to hurt you. I know you know that!"

Jim with his hat on backwards, stood up and straightened his hat up right. He pointed a finger at Miss Margie as he walked by her desk to Miss Brewster office. His finger waving up and down pointing at Miss Margie saying as he teased her.

JIM "I know you know that, I know you know that!"

As they walked in Miss Brewster's office. He smiles with satisfaction as she sat down behind her desk. She looked at Jim and pointed to a chair opposite her desk. Jim sat down, then turned his hat backwards again and folded his arms across his chest. Jim's first word out of his mouth was.

JIM "There's no more beds right, I know this system is messed up, you can send me back to Juvy (juvenile detention) right now!"

Jim's voice got louder Miss Brewster just watched him go through the motion of intimidation.

JIM "I know you people are just like the rest of them out there, right?"

Jim's finger pointing up and down at her.

JIM "I know you know that no one is gonna help a kid like me, right!"

Miss Brewster stood up and walked around to the front of her desk and sat on the edge of it, and looked at Jim. Miss Brewster said.

NOT TO GLORIFY BUT, ONLY TO IDENTIFY THOSE SITUATIONS IN THE HOODZ.

BREWSTER "We got one bed left and it's all yours if you want it."

Jim said as he folds his arms with his chin up high looking to one side carefully not to make eye contact.

JIM "Now thaz more like it!"

Miss Brewster just smiles and finish talking.

BREWSTER "But, there are two rules; #1 – you have to register for school with a counselor from here at the shelter. #2 – is that you go to church on Sundays."

Jim unfolded his arms and said.

JIM "Oh, no Miss Brewster, I don't play church, thaz not my thing. Homey don't play that!"

Miss Brewster surprised at his answer asked.

BREWSTER "Oh yeah, school don't scare

you, just church right?"

Jim quick thinking, then answered.

JIM "Naw, church don't scare me, it's the people thaz up in there that scare me."

Jim smiled with satisfaction once again. Miss Brewster held out her hand and Jim shook her hand, then she pointed to a door and said.

BREWSTER "You will be attending church right? Its 3 days before Sunday so make up your mind, ok?"

Jim stood up shaking his head no, but, he still walked toward the door. Then Miss Brewster said.

BREWSTER "On the second floor see Mr. Kake about bed #13."

Jim opened the door and walked up the stairs. Jim said in a stern voice as he entered the door on the second floor.

NOT TO GLORIFY BUT, ONLY TO IDENTIFY THOSE SITUATIONS IN THE HOODZ.

JIM "Who's Mr. Kake around this joint?"

Nobody stop talking they just kept on doing what they were doing. Then Jim stepped in front of bed #13. As he sized up the small cot type bed with a locker stamped #13 a tall man in a blue sweat suit with a graybeard came up to him and said.

KAKE "I'm Mr. Kake."

Jim stepped back looked him up and down and said.

JIM "If your beard was any grayer you would look like shady Grady on Sanford and Son."

Then Jim started to laugh.

JIM "Ha, ha, ha."

KAKE "Think so, well here's your bed sheets and pillow and theirs your locker.

NOT TO GLORIFY BUT, ONLY TO IDENTIFY THOSE SITUATIONS IN THE HOODZ.

See you in the morning son, also, lights out at 10:00pm."

As Jim sat down he mumbled out loud to Mr. Kake.

JIM "And I'm not your son, old man!"

Then Jim got up and opened his locker and hung his clothes up and put his hat on top of a book. Jim lift up his hat and took the book down and looked at it. (It was the Holy Bible) Jim looked around to see who was looking then he put the bible back and put his hat on top of it again and lay down and went to sleep.

(8am in Miss Brewster office)

As Jim walk in Miss Brewster's office, she spoke to him in a happy way.

BREWSTER "Good morning Jim."

Jim just stared at her then shook his head up and down in acknowledgement of her

NOT TO GLORIFY BUT, ONLY TO IDENTIFY THOSE SITUATIONS IN THE HOODZ.

statement.

BREWSTER "Our counselor will be here soon to go with you to register in school. I have all your records ready."

Then a knock came at the door. Miss Brewster said.

BREWSTER "Come in."

The door opened and Mr. Kake walked in. Jim eyes opened wide. Jim looked up at Miss Brewster then back at Mr. Kake and said.

JIM "I'm not goin to school with no old man! Nope, uh, uh, not me!"

Mr. Kake said.

KAKE "Good morning Miss Brewster."

Miss Brewster answered.

BREWSTER "Good morning Mr. Kake."

NOT TO GLORIFY BUT, ONLY TO IDENTIFY THOSE SITUATIONS IN THE HOODZ.

Then Mr. Kake looked over at Jim.

Mr. Kake said.

KAKE "Good morning son."

Miss Brewster gave Mr. Kake Jim's school records and then they left Miss Brewster's office. As they were driving along in the car Jim asked.

JIM "Why you keep callin me your son?"

Mr. Kake looked over at Jim and said.

KAKE "You never told me your name last night."

Jim said.

JIM "So, I'm still not your son."

Mr. Kake said.

KAKE "All you did is laugh at me for being old, so what do you expect me to act like or say to you?"

Jim looked at his hands and looked at Mr. Kake and said.

JIM "If someone don't like what I say, they got lightning and thunder to deal with!"

Then he balled up his left fist for lightning and his right fist for thunder. Mr. Kake then pulled up in front of the parking lot of the school.

Mr. Kake said.

KAKE "You know what Jim? I use to be just like that too."

As they got out of the car Jim looked over at Mr. Kake and said.

JIM "Man, you look like you been old all your life. You mean to tell me that you were once a kid!"

Then Jim rolled up his sleeves expecting Mr.
Kake to swing on him, but Mr. Kake was
smarter than that, he saw Jim's body language
and just smiled and shook his head and said.

KAKE "Come on son, let's go to the
counselor's office and see if we can get you back
in school. You know what Jim? I use to go to
this school too."

Jim looked shocked at what Mr. Kake said.
Then asked.

JIM "Are you serious? Only the slick, sly,
and wicked have gone to this school, you ain't
one of us!"

Mr. Kake just smiled again as they walked in
the front door. As they entered the principal's
office Mr. Kake greeted the counselor like they
have known each other for years. Mr. Kake
said.

NOT TO GLORIFY BUT, ONLY TO IDENTIFY THOSE SITUATIONS IN THE HOODZ.

KAKE "Good morning Mr. Jefferies."

Then Mr. Kake shook his hand. Mr. Jefferies answered.

JEFFERIES "Good morning Mr. Kake, and good morning Jim."

Jim just sat down and folded his arms across his chest. Mr. Jefferies said.

JEFFERIES "Well, in view of the situation as far as we are concern he'll have to do some major make up work, due to the fact of his loss of time, being out of school and all. But, I must add that his grades where..."

Jim interrupted as he unfolds his arms and said.

JIM "What you mean, putting me back, I worked hard when I was here. If it weren't for my mother, I wouldn't have stopped coming so don't be..."

NOT TO GLORIFY BUT, ONLY TO IDENTIFY THOSE SITUATIONS IN THE HOODZ.

Then Mr. Kake interrupted and said.

KAKE "So how were his grades Mr. Jefferies?" Mr. Jefferies said.

JEFFERIES "Oh yeah, this is what I was going to say."

As Mr. Jefferies spoke while looking in Jim's school records Mr. Kake motioned to Jim with his hand to be quiet. Mr. Jefferies continued on.

JEFFERIES "And his grades were exceptionally good for a child going through his trauma."

Mr. Kake interrupted and asked.

KAKE "Excuse me, what trauma?"

Mr. Jefferies said, "Didn't they tell you at the shelter?

Mr. Kake was caught off guard but then said.

KAKE "A little, so why don't you fill me in Mr. Jefferies."

Mr. Jefferies said.

JEFFERIES "Well, remember the situation you were in when you were about his age? 16 years old I think." Jim took off his hat and lowered his head and looked up at Mr. Kake.

KAKE "How could I forget."

JEFFERIES "Jim's mother died off of drugs and his father is incarcerated."

Mr. Kake said as he looked over at Jim.

KAKE "Yeah, my mother was shot and died, while my father was doing life in the penitentiary also. I also remember that if it wasn't for you and your bible study classes, I know I wouldn't have made it."

NOT TO GLORIFY BUT, ONLY TO IDENTIFY THOSE SITUATIONS IN THE HOODZ.

JEFFERIES "GOD is good isn't he?"

KAKE "Yes, all the time!" They both stood up and gave each other a five slap and then a holy hug.

Mr. Jefferies sat back down on the edge of his desk then said.

JEFFERIES "You see Jim, you're not the only one who's going through problems, or have been through something. Some are worse than others."

Jim looked up at Mr. Kake and wiped the sweat off his forehead as he held back the tears.

JEFFERIES "And Mr. Kake's attitude was a lot worse than yours. He also was a member of the K.A. Crew (kick ass crew) that ran the crap games and drugs in this school when I first came here, years ago."

Then Mr. Jefferies got up and said.

NOT TO GLORIFY BUT, ONLY TO IDENTIFY THOSE SITUATIONS IN THE HOODZ.

JEFFERIES "So, Jim let's get your schedule together so you can get started."

Mr. Kake shook Mr. Jefferies hand then he started for the door and peeped over his shoulder and said.

KAKE "See you later son."

Jim looked at him as he walked out of the counselor's office and lift up his hand to wave good bye but Mr. Kake back was toward him as he shut the door.

Later that morning in the classroom Jackee was saying with an attitude.

JACKEE "Whaz-up like that, cause you brothers ain't all that!"

As she shakes her head and finger pointing at Kent with her other hand on her hip. The sound of a drum beat from someone beating on his or her desktop as the step off begins. The class shouts. "Whaz-up, whaz-up, whaz-up like that?"

As the girls start steppin, Jackee starts rappin.

JACKEE "I turned the corner and saw this guy, he was taller than me almost reached the sky."

(Class shouted with an attitude.)

CLASS "Whaz-up, whaz-up, whaz-up like that?"

As all the girls joined in on Jackee's Rapp and stepped to the beat, the guys just stood there and wave their hands, then shook their heads, no-way! When the girls finished then Brenda started a conversation.

BRENDA "Why didn't you finish them off Jackee, cause you got skills girl!"

Jackee said in a slick way.

JACKEE "Cause they couldn't keep up if

they wanted too!"

All the girls started to laugh. Then Brenda said.

BRENDA "Ok, then wha-up whit Robert's father the junkie? Hey Jackee he keeps on askin me for a quarter every morning."

Then Tammy said.

TAMMY "Don't be supportin his habit!"

Jackee leaned over and tried to whisper to Brenda but, JoJo heard her.

JACKEE "I heard Roberts father was in the war and Robert was born when he came home. Also his father was infected with Agent green the nerve gas. Plus, he has a herron (heroine) problem."

Then JoJo stood up and said.

JOJO "Now see, thaz what I'm talkin bout,

why you sistas gotta be dishin the bruthas?"

Then Kent stood up and said.

KENT "Yeah, it's not his fault, it's in his blood, you art to try talkin to his fartha instead of putting Robert down!"

JoJo looked at Kent and said.

JOJO "Yeah, talk to the brutha!"

Saraj stood up and said.

SARAJ "Nobody said it's his fault; what, you left your miracle ear home? We talkin bout his fartha the bum! Ain't you heard dat!"

The drum beat started again as the class begin to say.

CLASS "Wha-up, wha-up, wha-up like that?"

Then Kent begin to rapp about its not his fault,

NOT TO GLORIFY BUT, ONLY TO IDENTIFY THOSE
SITUATIONS IN THE HOODZ.

the guys begin to step off.

GUYS "Did you ever ask him why he has an attitude? Did you ever ask him why he has no gratitude? He didn't just grow up to be a bum; he was his mutha's only son. When he came home from the war he was out on the street, one shoe on, one shoe off his feet!"

(Class holler.)

CLASS "Wha-up, wha-up, wha-up like that!"

As they came to the end of the step-off, someone standing by the door whispered.

GUY AT THE DOOR "Shh, shh, shhhh, here she comes, straighten up the desks and chairs ya'll hurry up, here she come."

Everybody move his or her chair back in place. Their teacher Miss Webster says with a smile as Jim follows her in the classroom.

NOT TO GLORIFY BUT, ONLY TO IDENTIFY THOSE SITUATIONS IN THE HOODZ.

WEBSTER "Good morning class, how are you today?"

And the class all started complaining at one time.

CLASS PEOPLE "My head hurts. My brother is sick can I leave? My dog ran away can I go look for him?"

As Miss Webster walked to her desk shaking her head with a smile she said.

WEBSTER "Class you remember Jim don't you? Well guess what, he's back."

Jim covered one side of his face from the teacher, smiled and made an ugly face at the class with his eyes criss cross. Kent raised his hand and Miss Webster asked.

WEBSTER "Yes, Kent?"

KENT "Miss Webster you asked how we doin, I don't feel so good, I think I got gas."

As his hand went under his arm pit and he squeezed it, there was a loud sound.

KENT "FART! FART! FART!"

Everybody laughed but the teacher. Then Miss Webster said with a straight face.

WEBSTER "Oh, we starting early today, if that's the case then everyone pass up their homework, right now! Hurry up."

Then Jackee raised her hand and said.

JACKEE "Miss Webster."

And Miss Webster answered.

WEBSTER "Yes Jackee."

Jackee said.

JACKEE "Miss Webster, my dog ate my homework last night."

NOT TO GLORIFY BUT, ONLY TO IDENTIFY THOSE
SITUATIONS IN THE HOODZ.

Jojo said out loud.

JOJO "Now why you callin you're little sista
a dog? Huh, wha-up like that?"

Brenda stood up and said.

BRENDA "Don't even go there!"

As she balled up her right fist then she shook
her head back and forth with the other hand on
her hip.

BRENDA "Why you gotta be pickin on my
girls like that?"

Kent stood up and said.

KENT "Cause the brutha got to watch what
we eat if we want to play ball."

Then he flexed his muscles as a big piece of
paper balled up like a baseball was thrown and
it bounced off his chest as he tried to catch it.

Everyone laughed as he sat back down embarrassed. Then Miss Webster said.

WEBSTER "Pass up your homework everyone, hurry, hurry, we don't have all day."

Jim was sitting down a few rows from Jackee and of course their eye contact was obvious to Saraj.

SARAJ "Why don't you go and switch seats with Kent and sit next to Jim so he can catch up on what we doin girl."

Kent heard that and said.

KENT "Oh you don't think I'm smart enough for Jim to learn from me?"

All the girls laughed and shook their heads at one time agreeing with what he said. Then Miss Webster turned around and starts writing on the black board.

NOT TO GLORIFY BUT, ONLY TO IDENTIFY THOSE
SITUATIONS IN THE HOODZ.

All of a sudden there was a lot of commotion outside the classroom down the hallway, and someone looked in the classroom and hollered.

GUY "Fight! Fight!"

Suddenly there was a stampede; everyone was racing to the door to see the fight. Miss Webster was the last to leave the classroom. As she walked behind the students the crowd opened up as she pushed the kids to one side. Miss Webster said as she tried to bring order to the crowd of students.

WEBSTER "Go to your classes, each of you get to your class!"

There were two guys, one on top of the other one, both fighting, swinging arms hitting each other. Then another teacher (Mr. Ross) came through the crowd; each teacher grabbed a boy.

One of the guys was Jackee's brother and he was the one on top of the other guy. When Jackee saw this she begins to push Mr. Ross telling him to let her little brother go.

Jackee said.

JACKEE "Hey you, let him go, before it's me and you! Let him go or I'll kick your butt!"

Jim looks on and stepped beside Jackee along with Kent, Saraj, Jojo, and Brenda. When Jackee said that, her little brother opened his mouth and screamed.

Mikee shouted.

MIKEE "Ok, ok, I'm alright Jackee, I'm alright!"

As Mr. Ross let his arm go Mikee brush off his pants leg and the front of his shirt with his hands and said.

MIKEE "See Jackee, look what you done girl! I had it under control but, naw, you had to jump in it, didn't you!"

NOT TO GLORIFY BUT, ONLY TO IDENTIFY THOSE SITUATIONS IN THE HOODZ.

Jackee said.

JACKEE "Yeah that's right, you know I don't play that. Somebody beatin up on you. What chu fightin him for anyhow?"

Mikee mumbled some words under his breath.

MIKEE "Over his hat."

Jackee said.

(SONG – ASK HIM WHY)

JACKEE "Wha-chu say speak up!"

Then Miss Webster let the other guy go, as the two teachers started to usher the other kids to their class. Jackee looked at Mikee and then looked at the other boy named Robert that he was fighting, then looked back at Mikee.

Jackee said.

JACKEE "Did he hurt you Mikee?"

NOT TO GLORIFY BUT, ONLY TO IDENTIFY THOSE
SITUATIONS IN THE HOODZ.

Mikee answered.

MIKEE "Naw, he couldn't hurt me even if I
let him!"
Then Jackee looked at the two teachers as they
continued to direct kids back to their classes.
Robert put his hat back on his head and begins
to brush off his clothes.

Jackee stepped over toward Robert, and then
Mikee stepped toward Robert. They both went
after him as they saw the teachers being
occupied. Jackee hit Robert in the chest he
threw up his guards.

Mikee knelt down behind him then she pushed
Robert over Mikee back and they both jumped
on Robert. The crowd of students came running
back. Jackee and Mikee were swinging on
Robert as he tried to backslide on the ground
trying to get up. All you could see was fist and
elbows flying everywhere.

Jackee and Mikee swinging forward and

NOT TO GLORIFY BUT, ONLY TO IDENTIFY THOSE
SITUATIONS IN THE HOODZ.

Robert swinging going backwards, somehow Robert broke free from all that swinging and got up with his hands covering his head and face, then he took off running down the hall. All the kids laughed at Robert.

Jim reached over and tapped Kent and said.

JIM "I don't remember Robert growing up around us."

Kent said.

KENT "Yeah, his mother tried to keep him in the house all the time so he wouldn't get hurt, that's sorta how he got hooked on drugs so fast. Cause she knew once he tried it he would be hooked cause his pop's was on it when he was born."

Jim said in a surprised voice.

JIM "Wha-chu talkin bout man?"

Kent said as he leaned over toward Jim.

NOT TO GLORIFY BUT, ONLY TO IDENTIFY THOSE SITUATIONS IN THE HOODZ.

KENT "You see man, it's in his blood, and his fartha is the bum that we always give money too, so he can eat."

Jim said.

JIM "Oh, you talkin bout the bum with one shoe on one shoe off his feet, the same guy I be tellin stories about."

Kent said

KENT "You got it man."

By then both teachers grabbed Jackee and Mikee then they waved the other kids to go on to class once again.

They all headed for the principal's office to get to the bottom of this situation. Mr. Ross said with a satisfying grin on his face.

ROSS "You're out of here this time Jackee!"

Miss Webster looked over at him squinting her
eye with a big smile and said.

WEBSTER "She'll come around, just wait
you'll see. It's her little brother I'm worried
about."

Jackee and Mikee looked at each other and
shrugged their shoulders. Mr. Ross looked at
Miss Webster smiled and said.

ROSS "That's what everybody keep telling
me!"

As they entered the school office Jackee and
Mikee looked at each other and sat down on a
bench outside the principal's office as the two
teachers went in to talk to the principal.

There were two people sitting there also, but
Jackee and Mikee were too busy discussing
their strategy plan for the principal's office to
notice. As they sat there waiting on their turn
Jackee begin to think about Mikee fighting over

a hat.

Jackee said.

JACKEE "Hey Mikee did we ever get that hat from Robert?"

Mikee said.

"Naw, cause after I started fightin him I realized that it didn't go with the color of my clothes that I got on."

Jackee stood up leaned back on both legs put her hands on her hips and said.

JACKEE "You mean to tell me that, in the middle of the fight you changed your mind about that hat?"

Mikee said.

MIKEE "Yeah Jackee but we had fun for a minute, we ain't fight in school in about a month now. I think we doin good, don't chu?"

NOT TO GLORIFY BUT, ONLY TO IDENTIFY THOSE
SITUATIONS IN THE HOODZ.

Jackee rolled her eyes and turned her head for one second then she jumped on Mikee as he slowly tried to get up from his seat. Jackee grabbed him by his collar and start shaking

him back and forth. Mikee said as he was being shaken.

MIKEE   "Thaz-why-I-didn't-want-you-to-jump-in-it!"

Each word after each shake, then Mikee bumped into the girl next to them.

CeCe said.

CECE "Hey watch it!"

Then she looked in amazement and asked.

CECE "Wow, how long you guys been sittin here?"

Jackee said in an angry voice.

JACKEE "I thought chu whaz in class, CeCe?"

CeCe said.

CECE "I was, till this girl start pulling my braids out!"

Then she rolled her eyes and folded her arms across her chest.

Mikee said.

MIKEE "Not again CeCe! Do you know how much money it cost momma for the lady to braid that fake hair girl?"

When CeCe heard that she jumped up threw her book at Mikee and began to throw punches at his chest screaming.

CECE "Shut up! Shut up, Mikee shut it up!"

NOT TO GLORIFY BUT, ONLY TO IDENTIFY THOSE SITUATIONS IN THE HOODZ.

Mikee was laughing the whole time as he takes each punch in the chest. Then Jackee pulled CeCe off Mike as the principal stepped up behind them shaking her head and pointing her finger toward her office door.

The principal Miss Alfiena said.

ALFIENA "Well, well, the whole family once again, what must I do to keep you kids from tearing this school apart? Come on in my office and let's talk."

Then principal Miss Alfiena called her secretary Miss Cheryl.

ALFIENA "Let the other student go back to their class and bring her three suspension forms."

CeCe jumped up and down pacing the floor saying.

CECE "Oh no, Miss Alfiena, none for me, it wasn't my fault this time, Lesley pulled my braids out when I wasn't looking."

As Miss Alfiena closed her office door with all of them gathered in her office then She said.

ALFIENA "Miss Cheryl also page for Robert, Lesley, and Terry please."

CeCe raised her hand and spoke up.

CECE "Oh yeah, it also was Terri too."

Miss Alfiena said.

ALFIENA "Don't you kids know by now there's nothing that the kids in this school do that I don't know about?"

Mikee leaned over to Jackee and whispered.

MIKEE "It must be expensive paying all those snitchers."

Miss Alfiena looked over at Mikee as she peeped over the top of her classes and said.

NOT TO GLORIFY BUT, ONLY TO IDENTIFY THOSE
SITUATIONS IN THE HOODZ.

ALFIENA "Speak up Mikee, I can't hear
you?"

Mikee then said.

MIKEE "I said, I got a wedgee in my
britches!"

Just in time to save the day, Miss Cheryl
knocked on the door and came in with the
paper work. Miss Judy and Miss Webster
followed, and then came Mr. Ross and Lesley.
Before they knew it, in came Terry and Robert.

Robert had a band-aide on the side of his face,
and his hand was also bandaged up. As they all
stood in front of Miss Alfiena, Lesley kicked
CeCe, Jackee popped Lesley upside the back of
her head; Terry hit CeCe on the arm, Mikee
pinched Terry's arm.

Robert elbowed Mikee in the side; Miss
Webster stomped Robert's toe. All this was
going on by the time Mr. Ross explained the

fight to Miss Alfiena, then Miss Judy spoke up
about CeCe, Lesley, and Terry.

Miss Judy said in a stern voice.

JUDY "I blamed CeCe for allowing these
girls to play with her braids!"

CeCe shouted.

CECE "I didn't let them play with it, they
pulled my braids and I told you that! and you
said,"

As CeCe imitated Miss Judy by shaking her
head and putting her hands on her hips.

CECE "Stop playing with your hair CeCe!"

Then Robert spoke up about how Mikee wanted
to wear his hat in school and he told him no.

ROBERT "Uh, Mikee, uh, asked me could
he wear uh, my hat. Uh, I said no. Uh, Mikee
starts hittin me, uh, so I hit him back. I walked

away, uh, before I knew it he jumped on me and
we, uh, fell to the ground fightin. Uh, thaz all I
have to say."

Mikee stepped toward Robert and said.

MIKEE "Uh, can you shut up Robert, you
on drugs anyway? Uh, you only gonna end up
ten years from now on that drug called ICE any
way; watch, it's gonna catch up with you man!"

Robert looked at Mikee then looked at the floor,
put his hands in his pockets and said.

ROBERT "Yeah right, uh, I'm way to cool
for that. Uh, can we go now Miss Alfiena?"

Miss Alfiena said.

ALFIENA "Ok, everybody out!"

As CeCe, Mikee and Jackee tried to go through
the door Miss Alfiena peeped over her classes as
she was writing all this confusion down and
said.

NOT TO GLORIFY BUT, ONLY TO IDENTIFY THOSE
SITUATIONS IN THE HOODZ.

ALFIENA "Wait a minute you three, we
need to talk, close the door after everyone else
leave."

Then Lesley and Terry licked their tongue out
at CeCe as Mikee tried to shut them up in the
door as he closed it.

Miss Alfiena said.

ALFIENA "Look kids, you have a month
and a half left before school ends. All three of
you are going to make it, once Mikee pulls his
math grade up. I'm going to send all three of
you home for the rest of the day. When you
come back tomorrow and if I hear one of your
names mentioned in the next 45 days you're out
of here for good! Do we understand each
other?"

Kids all together said.

MIKEE, JACKEE, AND CECE "Yes Miss
Alfiena."

NOT TO GLORIFY BUT, ONLY TO IDENTIFY THOSE
SITUATIONS IN THE HOODZ.

Miss Alfiena said.

ALFIENA "Now go, I'll see you tomorrow
and I'll tear these papers up; also, I will be
calling your mother tonight and let her know
today's outcome."

Mikee, Jackee, and CeCe, said at the same time.

MIKEE, JACKEE, AND CECE "Yes Miss
Alfiena."

Mikee shut the door and smiled at Miss Cheryl
as he grabbed an apple off her desk and said.

MIKEE "Looks good enough to eat."

Miss Cheryl held out her hand as she stood up
and pats her feet waiting for Mikee to return
her apple. Then he smiled and sat the apple
back down and begins to rhyme. Mikee sounds
out in a song.

MIKEE "Fiena, fiena, bo fiena, bo nanna

NOT TO GLORIFY BUT, ONLY TO IDENTIFY THOSE
SITUATIONS IN THE HOODZ.

fanna fo fiena, fe-fi o meana; Alfiena."

As they left the office CeCe waved bye to Miss
Cheryl. Jackee's brother and sister walked
ahead of her saying the name rhyme again only
this time for Miss Cheryl. Mikee and Jackee
said.

MIKEE AND JACKEE "Now let's say
Cheryl, Cheryl bo feryl, bo nanna fanna fo
feryl, fe-fi o- meryl, cher-ryl."

Miss Cheryl stood there with a smile on her face
waving them to hurry up and leave the office.
Then the three of them grabbed each other's
waist and one behind another and stepped
together as they walked out the office rhyming
Alfiena and Cheryl.

Miss Cheryl waved harder ushering them out
the door while she laughed. After school that
evening Jim walked into the shelter with a sad
look on his face as he wonders what is going to
happen to Jackee. As he lay the pile of books on
his bed, he sits down, hang his head down then

**looks up. He hears the conversation the guys
across from the lockers were having.**

First guy read out loud.

**FIRST GUY "We have accepted your
application at our place of employment and
would like for you to start next Monday at
9:00am."**

**The second guy jumped up off the bed and
raised his hand for a high five and said.**

SECOND GUY "Praise the Lord!"

Both hands smacked together.

First guy said.

FIRST GUY "Thank you Jesus!"

**Then he walked over to two other guys and
read the letter. Jim heard another guy say,**

OTHER GUY "Got to give GOD the glory!"

Jim stood up and walked to his locker and mumbled to himself.

JIM "Yeah GOD you always help others, well you keep right on helping them cause, I don't need you. Shoot, wha-chu done for me anyhow?"

Jim took his hat off and put it on the shelf. The bible was still there so Jim took it in his hand and turned around to take it somewhere else and there was Mr. Kake standing there looking at Jim books on the bed.

Jim said.

JIM "Wha-chu need old man?"

Mr. Kake said.

KAKE "Do you need some help with your work son?"

Jim said in a sarcastic way.

NOT TO GLORIFY BUT, ONLY TO IDENTIFY THOSE
SITUATIONS IN THE HOODZ.

JIM "Wha-chu think?"

Mr. Kake walked away shaking his head.

Mr. Kake said.

KAKE "See your later son."

Jim still had the bible in his hand as he sat back
down. A guy walked over to his bed and said.

GUY "Is your name Jim?"

Jim smiled at the question then answered.

JIM "Yeah, that's me."

Then the guy said.

GUY "Man, I heard you are death with your
hands, and I heard when you put your heart
into it you are the man with all the answers in
the streets."

NOT TO GLORIFY BUT, ONLY TO IDENTIFY THOSE
SITUATIONS IN THE HOODZ.

Jim lifts up his left fist then his right fist and
said.

JIM "With lightnin and thunda I can't
miss!"

Then the guy took his hands from behind his
back and there was a bible in his hands, he
opened it and said.

GUY "What's this word in Deuteronomy,
chapter7, verse 7?"

Then the guy spelled out the word f e w e s t.
Jim didn't open the bible he had in his hand. He
got up looked at the guy's bible as he pointed to
the word and Jim answered.

JIM "Fewest of all people."

Then Jim looked up at verse 5, then he starts
reading. When he got to verse 6 the guy closed
the book then said.

GUY "Thanks man, you are all right."

NOT TO GLORIFY BUT, ONLY TO IDENTIFY THOSE SITUATIONS IN THE HOODZ.

He gave Jim a high five and then he shouted.

GUY "PRAISE THE LORD!"

Then he walked away. Jim felt an electric charge go all over his body. Jim's body shook from head to toe. Finally, he sat down, opened the bible he had in his hand. Just then the bell rang for dinner. Jim closed it as fast as he opened it, got up put the bible back in his locker and went to dinner. Jim was the last to leave the room, he looked back at the empty room and hollered.

JIM "JESUS!"

Then he looked around to see if anything would happen, then he strolled down to the dining room for dinner.

(MEANWHILE)

At the house washing dishes before their

NOT TO GLORIFY BUT, ONLY TO IDENTIFY THOSE SITUATIONS IN THE HOODZ.

mother came home; Jackee washing, Mikee drying, CeCe putting them away CeCe said.

CECE "What we gonna tell Momma-Tanya?"

Jackee said.

JACKEE "First we say that you CeCe had a problem with Terry and Lesley and when me and Mikee came to help you the boy Robert jumped in it."

CeCe said with a discussed look on her face.

CECE "Uh, uh, nope, thaz lying!"

Mikee said.

MIKEE "Yeah, CeCe its either lie or butt whippin, the last time Momma-Tanya beat us you cried so loud that the birds were on the window seal rappin to your cryin. TWEET, TWEET, TWEET, TWEET,"

CeCe put down the plate and went after Mikee with her fist balled up ready to fight. Jackee grabbed a hand full of her dish water and threw some on the both of them. Then she stepped between them.

Jackee said.

JACKEE "Calm down ya'll! Wha-up like that? Can't we all, just get along?"

Mikee and CeCe looked at Jackee and then they jumped on her. Mikee used the towel he was drying dishes with to hit Jackee. CeCe grabbed Jackee by the arm and tried to swing her around as Jackee made it look like CeCe had great strength.

Just then the front door opened up and there was their mother stepping fast as usual, calling out orders as if she had a check list going down and checking each chore off. Momma-Tanya said in a rushed voice.

MOMMA-TANYA "Did you do the beds, the

dishes, sweep the floor, and take out the trash?"

As Jackee and Mikee grabbed their mothers arm, CeCe fluffed up the pillow in the lounge wooden rocking chair, and points to it inviting their mother to sit down.

Jackee on one side, Mikee on the other and CeCe kneeling down looking up at her while putting on her slippers. Jackee spoke first trying to ease up the tension that's about to come when that phone call come through from the principal.

JACKEE "Momma-Tanya, now you know it's time to talk about you and these jobs you workin, I'm tired of watchin you go through all this stress!"

Momma-Tanya said with a smile, then came a worried look across her face.

MOMMA-TANYA "Now, you kids know I only have one hour before I have to go to my next job but I'm glad you sat me down I got some good news and some bad news."

CeCe jumped up with a worried look on her face and said.

CECE "You not gonna go to war and die like daddy did, are you? Are you? I don't want to lose you too!"

Then she grabbed her mother and hugged her real tight. Momma-Tanya said.

MOMMA-TANYA "No child, who been putting those thoughts in your head? Not at all, I'm not leaving you. I've had an offered to go to school by my first job, to upgrade my computer skills.

Then they will promote me to supervisor depending on my grades in school. It's only for 90 days starting this summer when you get out of school and ends when you go back."

Mikee said with a big smile.

NOT TO GLORIFY BUT, ONLY TO IDENTIFY THOSE SITUATIONS IN THE HOODZ.

MIKEE "This means you'll quit your second job and just work one, right?"

Momma-Tanya answered.

MIKEE "Yes Michael, that is correct."

Jackee jumped up and hollered.

JACKEE "Yesss!"

Momma-Tanya said without a smile.

MOMMA-TANYA "My only problem is, to concentrate in school for the summer. I need you kids on a tight schedule or send you down the country to visit your GRANDMOMMA and granddaddy for the summer."

CeCe jumped up just like Jackee did when she heard the news, and hollered.

CECE "Yesss!"

Then Mikee shouted along with Jackee.

NOT TO GLORIFY BUT, ONLY TO IDENTIFY THOSE
SITUATIONS IN THE HOODZ.

MIKEE AND JACKEE "Nooo!"

Momma-Tanya said.

MOMMA-TANYA "Now, let's get dinner together so I can get started for my part-time job."

Just then the phone rang. "RING, RING" As their mother grabbed for the phone Jackee, Mikee, and CeCe said out loud.

JACKEE, MIKEE, AND CECE "I'll get it!"

Momma-Tanya picked up the phone and said.

MOMMA-TANYA "Hello, oh hi, how are you doing? Oh yeah, that was expensive hair they braided on CeCe's hair. Huh, what! Oh yeah, oh they did, did they? I understand, well you take care and may God Bless you, good bye."

As Momma-Tanya talked on the phone Jackee,

NOT TO GLORIFY BUT, ONLY TO IDENTIFY THOSE SITUATIONS IN THE HOODZ.

Mikee and CeCe start walking backwards away from her, as she hung up the phone.

Momma-Tanya said.

MOMMA-TANYA "So where were we, what you kids want to eat?"

They all looked each other in disbelief that their mother said nothing. Jackee hollered with a smile on her face (a sigh of relief).

JACKEE "Hotdogs!"

Mikee hollered.

MIKEE "Cheese burgers!"

CeCe said in a sorta quiet voice.

CECE "Veggies with no meat."

Momma-Tanya just laughed and said.

MOMMA-TANYA "So be it."

NOT TO GLORIFY BUT, ONLY TO IDENTIFY THOSE
SITUATIONS IN THE HOODZ.

Her kids smiled as they looked at each other
and listened to their mother humming a church
song as she got up from the chair.

((MEANWHILE back at the shelter)

(SONG – TO THE LIGHT)

After Jim ate dinner, he was sitting on his bed
doing his school homework he fell asleep. Mr.
Kake walked by Jim's bed, collected the books
from Jim's bed and sat them on the floor, then
walked away. A few minutes later Mr. Kake
announced over the intercom.

KAKE "Lights out, its 10:00pm."

The next day was Tuesday and Jim studied,
Wednesday night Jim studied, Thursday night
Jim studied. Late Thursday night about
12:30am Jim got up to go to the bathroom and
while he was coming back from there he heard
whispering coming from in back of the lockers.

NOT TO GLORIFY BUT, ONLY TO IDENTIFY THOSE
SITUATIONS IN THE HOODZ.

As he walked toward the lockers he saw 3 or 4 flash lights shining down. Then as he got closer one light shined on him, then another. Jim held up his hands as the light blinded him. Someone pulled his arm down and his body followed. When he sat down someone shined a light on the bible that was being passed to him, then a deep voice said.

DEEP VOICE "Read chapter 7 verse 9, 10, and 11 of Deuteronomy.

As Jim vision focused in on the verses he began to read, verse 9, 10, 11, 12, and 13.

Then the voice said.

VOICE "If you hungry come back tomorrow!"

The flashlights went out, and someone lifted the book from Jim's hand and everyone got up and went to their beds. Jim laid down on his bed and heard whispers of people saying the Lord's prayer.

Before they finished Jim in the dark got up and knelt down beside his bed until the prayer was finished, then they all got in bed. Jim woke up fresh and ready for the world the next morning, and went to school confident of his studies.

He had his first three tests that day in Math, English and the other in geography. The next day Jim had collected his test papers from each class. His face lit up like the fireworks from the fourth of July.

There was a bright glow as he smiled when he looked at each paper from each class. The rest of his day was a breeze, he went to each class and his chest stuck out with the boldness of an eagle as it stalked its prey.

That night Jim entered the shelter with a smile, he had his test papers in one hand, and his books under his arm. He just had to tell someone here about his accomplishment or he would explode. Just like at school, he often showed off his papers that day. Then Jim spotted a guy sitting on his bed.

Jim walked over and said.

JIM "Look my brother, look at these grades."

As Jim handed him the papers, the guy looked at the papers and smiled, then threw up a hand for a high five. The guy said out loud.

GUY "Praise the Lord!"

Jim walked away and all of a sudden words from nowhere came from out of his mouth.

JIM "Thank you JESUS!"

Jim looked around in surprise of himself, as if someone else had said those words. Then Jim spotted Kent and Jojo who had stopped by the shelter to congratulate him on his grades. Jim left so early after school that they didn't get a chance to holler (talk to him) at him.

NOT TO GLORIFY BUT, ONLY TO IDENTIFY THOSE
SITUATIONS IN THE HOODZ.

Then Jim said.

JIM "My brothers let me show you something."

Kent and Jojo looked at each other with amazement of how Jim conversation has begun to change, from, "Man" to "Bruther."

Jim put his books in his locker then took off his shirt and hung it up. Took his bible off the shelf put his hat in its place then sat on the side of his bed and opened it up. He begins to explain Deuteronomy to Kent and Jojo.

Jim had always been a good storyteller and that's how he kept their interest. He would act out with feelings and body language as he read the scripture and together they begin to learn a little at a time about the bible.

(A month went by and all is well)

At the last day of school in the hallway CeCe running; Lesley and Terry right behind her, she

spotted Jackee, Brenda, Tammy, and Saraj and
ran around them as Lesley and Terry were still
chasing her.

Saraj asked.

SARAJ "Wha-up little sista? Want me to
take care of your light work?"

CeCe in between breathes, as she slowed down
to duck around Saraj.

CeCe said

CECE "Naw, I got it under control."

Tammy said.

TAMMY "Turn around CeCe and kick their
butt!"

Then Brenda said.

BRENDA "Hey Jackee how about I just
teach your sista how to box, ok!"

NOT TO GLORIFY BUT, ONLY TO IDENTIFY THOSE SITUATIONS IN THE HOODZ.

Then CeCe said.

CECE "Naw, hhh, hhh, (gasping for breath) I got this under control."

Jackee said.

JACKEE "CeCe can't stand to watch someone bleed!"

Jackee looked at Saraj and Brenda as she winked one eye. Then she pointed at Terry and Lesley. CeCe in between breathes blurted out.

CECE "Yeah, I hate to have to hit somebody in the nose and they start bleeding!"

Just then Lesley and Terry stopped running after CeCe and caught their breath.

Lesley said.

LESLEY "I'll get you when you go to the store for your momma!"

NOT TO GLORIFY BUT, ONLY TO IDENTIFY THOSE
SITUATIONS IN THE HOODZ.

Then Terry looked at CECE with fist balled up
and said.

TERRY "Yeah, we'll be waitin for you
chump!"

Tammy with an attitude said.

TAMMY "Want me to kick one of them for
you CeCe?"

As Lesley and Terry begin to walk away in a
hurry CeCe stepped out from behind Jackee.

Tammy said.

TAMMY "You definantly need a new
attitude girl!"

Then Tammy put her hand on one hip as she
pointed at CeCe. Then CeCe balled up her fist
and shouted.

CECE "Yeah, next time I'm gonna box you

up! Blood or no blood! Don't make me bust you up!"

Brenda said.

BRENDA "Jackee, what days we gonna practice for the back to school talent show in September before school open back up?"

Jackee said.

JACKEE "I don't know I think we gonna have to cancel the group this year. Momma-Tanya thinkin bout sendin us down the country with GRANDMOMMA and granddaddy."

Tammy said.

TAMMY "Oh, no not the country again!"

Brenda said.

BRENDA "Last time you went, three years ago, you came back with pig tails and tight jeans."

NOT TO GLORIFY BUT, ONLY TO IDENTIFY THOSE SITUATIONS IN THE HOODZ.

Saraj said.

SARAJ "Yeah, and you were talkin funny too!"

CeCe said.

CECE "Here comes Mikee. Jackee check his report card and see if he failed math."

Mikee walked over to them with his head held down and reached out with his report card to hand it to Jackee then said.

MIKEE "I'm sorry Jackee, and CeCe but, I couldn't do it, I had to show them guys in my class that I ain't no dummy. I passed my math class."

Then Mikee looked at Jackee and then CeCe hollered out loud.

CECE "Yesss!"

NOT TO GLORIFY BUT, ONLY TO IDENTIFY THOSE
SITUATIONS IN THE HOODZ.

Then Jackee said to Mikee with both fist balled
up and her eyes watering up getting ready to
cry but, the anger took over.

JACKEE "Out of all the times you be fakin,
now you want even go to summer school for us.
I don't understand you Mikee, you could have
failed that class with no problem if you wanted
too, and you were our last hope."

Jackee looked at Mikee with those beady eyes as
tears begin to flow down her cheek. Then CeCe
called her.

CECE "Jackee, Jackee, we are out for the
summer, let's go home."

CeCe start pulling on Jackee's arm. Just then
Jim, Jojo and Kent walked up and they all start
walking home together. As CeCe continue to
hold on to Jackee, Mikee kinda backed up a
little as if to fall behind the crowd.

Then Brenda and Saraj begin to sing a song to
calm Jackee down as she looked over her

shoulder to see where her brother Mikee was. Then Jim walked up to Jackee on the other side of the arm that was free and begin to hold Jackee's hand as they walked and sang together. Jackee looked at Jim with a blushing smile.

(THREE DAYS LATER)

Jackee on one line, Saraj at home on the 2nd line. Tammy down stairs at Brenda house and Brenda upstairs on the 3rd line of the three-way phone hookup. Jackee said,

JACKEE "Momma-Tanya is shippin us out tomorrow morning."

Saraj said.

SARAJ "Yeah, don't your Momma-Tanya know that Frankie is givin a party tomorrow night?"

Tammy said.

TAMMY "Don't be stupid Saraj!"

Brenda said.

**BRENDA "Yeah, wha-up like that Saraj?
Wha would your Momma say if she knew you
were goin!"**

They all giggled over the phone. Then Jackee
said.

**JACKEE "Don't forget while I'm down the
country I need each of you to call each night.
Then I can go over the new songs and steps I'll
be writin and puttin down in my letters to
ya'll."**

Saraj said with her Jamaican accent.

**SARAJ "Don't wu-rry my sista I keep them
sistas in check!"**

Then Tammy jealously said.

NOT TO GLORIFY BUT, ONLY TO IDENTIFY THOSE
SITUATIONS IN THE HOODZ.

TAMMY "Yeah right little sista, who died
and made you boss?"

Brenda said.

BRENDA "Yeah, who made you chief,
chump!"

Saraj said with a smile.

SARAJ "Ya'll wouldn't be sayin that if I was
over there."

Brenda said.

BRENDA "Ain't my fault your pop's putting
you to work in the morning on the yard, cutting
grass."

Tammy said.

TAMMY "Tote that bar, and lift that bale!"

Then they all laughed over the phone as Tammy
put some base in her voice to sound like a man.

Then Mikee stepped in front of Jackee and pointed at his watch letting her know it's time to get off the phone.

Jackee said.

JACKEE "Yeah, I gotta go cause Mikee starin down my throat. You sistas take care and I'll see you in a couple of months, and don't forget to call and write."

Everybody said good bye and hung up the phone. Then Mikee picked up the phone and dialed some numbers.

MIKEE "Wha-up is Jojo home? Oh, he's at the rec. center, alright tell 'em Mikee called."

Then Mikee dialed again to call someone else, he got no answer. Mikee hung up the phone then, CeCe and Momma-Tanya walked in the room.

Momma-Tanya said.

NOT TO GLORIFY BUT, ONLY TO IDENTIFY THOSE SITUATIONS IN THE HOODZ.

MOMMA-TANYA "Ok kids it's time for bed."

Mikee said.

MIKEE "But, I just got on the phone."

Jackee said.

JACKEE "And nobody's home either."

As she begins to snicker (little laugh with her hands covering her mouth), then Momma-Tanya looked at Jackee and she stopped.

CeCe while rubbing her eyes said.

CECE "I'm ready to go to bed, I want to get up early."

Then she begins to stretch her arms out with a yarn at the same time Jackee said.

JACKEE "Who asked you all that, CeCe?"

NOT TO GLORIFY BUT, ONLY TO IDENTIFY THOSE SITUATIONS IN THE HOODZ.

As Jackee begin to stomp out the room disappointed, her brother mumbled.

MIKEE "CeCe keep your thoughts to yourself!"

CeCe asked.

CECE "What did I say? What I say?"

Then she looked around for someone to answer her.

Momma-Tanya said.

MOMMA-TANYA "Jackee come here, baby girl. I know you haven't been to stay with GRANDMOMMA and granddaddy in a while. It's a blessing that they are still alive cause they've been through a lot in their lifetime. You need to know who you are and who's you are. No one can explain it to you better than your grandparents."

Mikee said.

NOT TO GLORIFY BUT, ONLY TO IDENTIFY THOSE SITUATIONS IN THE HOODZ.

MIKEE "I know who I am!"

Jackee said.

JACKEE "Me too! Momma-Tanya we just want to stay here and take care of you."

Making their last plea before tomorrow comes.

Mikee said.

MIKEE "Yeah, Momma-Tanya we wouldn't let you down."

CeCe said.

CECE "Momma-Tanya can I go to bed now?"

Jackee grabbed CeCe by the hand and led her out the room with Mikee following them saying.

MIKEE "We'll be right back Momma-Tanya."

NOT TO GLORIFY BUT, ONLY TO IDENTIFY THOSE
SITUATIONS IN THE HOODZ.

Momma-Tanya just smiled as she picked one of
the suitcases up and put it by the doorway.

(IN THE MORNING A TAXI CAB
HONKED ITS HORN)

Jackee said.

JACKEE "Mikee don't you forget your
church belt."

Then Mikee answered.

MIKEE "I won't. Hey CeCe don't forget
your church socks."

Then CeCe answered.

CECE "I won't. Momma-Tanya, don't
forget our hugs and kisses."

Momma-Tanya answered.

MOMMA-TANYA "I won't. Jackee, don't

forget your slip for your church dress."

Then Jackee looked over at Momma-Tanya and said with an attitude.

JACKEE "Wha-up like that? Why I got to be wearin a slip under that dress? It's not like there any boys down there. Ain't nothin but, old men and women down there?"

Momma-Tanya said.

MOMMA-TANYA "Who you think you talkin too!"

Jackee thought for a second and then looked over at her mother with a blank expression, then smiled and said.

JACKEE "Sorry momma, I'll get the slip."

CeCe with her arms opened wide waving everyone to come together.

CECE "Smooches and hugs everybody."

NOT TO GLORIFY BUT, ONLY TO IDENTIFY THOSE
SITUATIONS IN THE HOODZ.

As they hugged one another in a big circle, Momma-Tanya begin to say a prayer for them as she put a little melody with it.

MOMMA-TANYA "Lord, shield my children from all hurt harm and danger as they travel to their grandparent's house. And keep them on one accord to do your good will, touch their hearts, minds and spirit with your good news that Jesus is our Lord and Savior, Amen."

They all picked up bags and suitcases and opened the door and walked toward the cab to begin their journey to their grandparent's house. As the cab pulled up in front of their grandparent's house Mikee begin to mumble to himself.

MIKEE "I hope she got enough to pay for this cab."

CeCe yawned, then she said.

CECE "Boy, Momma-Tanya already paid

the cab driver, Daaaaa!"

CeCe looked at Mikee then rolled her eyes at him.

Mikee said.

MIKEE "I knew that! I was just waking up talkin in my sleep."

As he hurried up and opened the door to get out the cab to avoid any more criticism from his two sisters he looked up at the house.

"SLAM" went the screen door, and out came their grandmomma running with open arms towards them. Before she got to them granddaddy appeared at the door shaking his head from embarrassment then he slowly followed her.

Then Jackee and CeCe got out the cab and just stared at them in amazement of how energetic they were. CeCe just smiled and threw out both arms to hug her grandmomma while Jackee headed for the trunk of the cab to collect their luggage and Mikee followed behind her.

Then their Granddaddy said

GRANDDADDY "Let me get those bags for ya'll."

Mikee said.

MIKEE "I got it granddaddy!"

Mikee trying to show his granddad that he was a big boy now. Then his granddaddy stopped in his tracks and begins to smile at Mikee and Jackee in amazement of how big they both have grown.

As their granddaddy reached out to get a piece of their luggage he also grabbed Mikee all in one swoop. Jackee burst out laughing as Mikee and the bags of luggage went up in the air.

Their granddaddy was medium build medium height, wasn't too heavy, about 180lbs, short

haircut clean shaved and light brown skin.
Their GRANDMOMMA on the other hand was
built like a black stallion.

She had a stocky build, hips that stood out,
broad shoulders and coal black hair that shined
in the sun light. Like a diamond that glittered
when put in front of a light, which made her
hair look rich and silky smooth.

She often leaned back on her legs as if she was a
proud bird over her nest of eggs. Then
grandmomma asked Jackee to get the bags and
CeCe ran over to Jackee to help, then
grandmomma leaned back on her legs (in a
rocking motion) with her hands on her hips and
said.

GRANDMOMMA "What's this, is my little
Jackee all grown up now, or, is my eyes deceivin
me?"

Then Jackee begin to blush as she looked over
at her GRANDMOMMA. The memories begin
to form in Jackee's mind her hard expression of

the city begin to melt.

Then Jackee ran to her with open arms.

Grandmomma said.

GRANDMOMMA "What's this?"

As her face glowed in the sunlight; then Jackee
answered.

JACKEE "Grandmomma, I almost didn't
come, I wanted to stay home with my friends so
bad."

The tears just came down as a sign of relief.

CeCe looked at Jackee and smiled, while Mikee
kept on asking his granddaddy to put him
down. He walked toward the house with bags in
one arm and Mikee in the other.

Grandmomma said.

GRANDMOMMA "Praise the Lord honey,

that's GOD's way of letting you know, that it's
time."

Mikee yelled out.

MIKEE "Time for what grandmomma?"

As granddaddy carried him up the steps
through the front door. The cab drove off and
grandmomma and the girls walked up the steps
into the house as their grandmomma begin to
explain.

GRANDMOMMA "There's always a
battle when it comes down to right or wrong,
you have to choose between the two. The good
news is that GOD is with you no matter what
choice you make."

CeCe said,

CECE "Well Momma-Tanya made her come
whether she liked it or not!"

NOT TO GLORIFY BUT, ONLY TO IDENTIFY THOSE
SITUATIONS IN THE HOODZ.

Mikee said.

MIKEE "Be quiet CeCe!"

Mikee said as granddaddy finally put him down
and they begin to go back outside to get the rest
of the bags.

When Mikee and granddaddy came back with
the last of the bags Mikee said.

MIKEE "Man, I thought ya'll were about
eighty years old by now."

Grandmomma looked over at granddaddy and
smiled then asked him.

GRANDMOMMA "Granddaddy, bout how
old is we now?"

Granddaddy put the bags down grabbed his
back and start waking slow with a limp and
said.

GRANDDADDY "Yeah, Grandmomma I

think we's bout eighty-two years ole, now help me find my walkin cane. Cause you'd know I can't see too well with these ole glasses on, let alone walk to well without my walkin cane."

They all start laughing and begin to set the table for breakfast. As they all sat down to eat granddaddy said.

GRANDDADDY "Well, the answer to ya'll question is that, we are only as old as we feel. I'm feelin bout seventy-three and Grandmomma is feelin about seventy-two."

CeCe shouted.

CECE "WOW!"

Jackee said.

JACKEE "I sure hope I look and feel like you when I get that old."

Mikee said.

NOT TO GLORIFY BUT, ONLY TO IDENTIFY THOSE SITUATIONS IN THE HOODZ.

MIKEE "Me too!"

Grandmomma said.

GRANDMOMMA "Well, our secret is EXERCISE AND PRAYER. Now granddaddy bless the food so's we can eat, cause ya'll look like you could stand some meat on them bones of yours."

Through the Whole summer the kids were motivated by their grandparents. With exercise and prayer day and night this gave them a sense of being, through the revelation of GOD to know there is a GOD who loves them.

This summer was not like any other summer they ever had before. It was like their mind, body, and spirit were touched by GOD himself. They didn't talk the same nor did they act the same.

It was like their thoughts were generated by the power of the HOLLY SPIRIT. And, to top it off, there was a history lesson of how they

became who they are. It took the whole summer for their granddaddy to tell the story, he would tell a little each night.

Their granddaddy would speak out boldly and proud as he told the story that summer. Granddaddy told the beginning of their family tree of where they come from, like it was told to him.

GRANDDADDY "He washed me white as snow, let go, and let GOD! He picked me up, and turned me around, put my feet, on solid ground! He showed me the way, only to live for this day. For this is our story and only by GOD's GRACE am I here today!"

Their Granddaddy said this with a big smile on his face, proud, bold, and serious as he could be, he told them the story only, just because. To know who they are, they had to know who's they are.

Grandmomma came in the living room each night with a cup of hot tea with herbs and spices in them that calmed even Mikee the energetic of the three. As she sat down with everybody she always hummed a special tune as granddaddy told the story.

(TELLING THE STORY OF MISS HAZEL AKA MISS H; THEIR GREAT, GREAT, GREAT, GRANDMOTHER WAS ON A COTTON FARM AS A SLAVE.)

Master PERVIS walks in the shack cursin and swearin, while drawin his whip in the air, ready to strike all in the same breath.

PERVIS "I swear if I told you once I've told you before, to get you butt up off them their knees of yours and get to the fields! Or I'll whip the black hide off your tail!"

Miss H as she was called back in those days said.

MISS H "I woke up late this morning."

She says in a soft and shaky voice as she stops in

the middle of her praying on her knees.
Then she turns and looks up at him as the whip
comes down on her upper back and shoulder.

Master PERVIS said.

PERVIS "It don't matter how much you
pray no one's gonna save you! Look at you, half
naked on your knees. Others want work
without you being there. I'll have to kill them.
So, you get up, dag on it. Or you'll get another
taste of my whip."

As he raises the whip a second time, the clash of
flesh against the whip sounds like a smack as if
a new born baby was being smacked on the butt
to bring life to it. Then she stands up to face the
wall to brace herself, not to fall as she screams
out loud.

MISS H "JESUS, help me lord! Come by her
O'lord!"

The crowd outside her shack stands in line with
heads hung down as Miss H. screams is muffled

to a murmur as she takes the whipping. Minutes later as she appears from the shack draping her cloth shawl over her shoulders.

Blood and tears roll down her cheek, as the crack of the whip echoes in her ears. Then she goes beyond the pain to say.

MISS H "Jesus will fix it, thaz wha GOD said!"

As the whip crack again she steps in the crowd, and they all begin to march to the fields. Then she begins to say out loud as if to be singing.

MISS H "Jesus will fix it, thaz wha GOD said, GOD said it! Jesus will deliver us, thaz wha GOD said, GOD said it!"

As they marched on, the crowd mumbles along with her and they begin to get louder as if to be motivated by her words.

The crowd said.

NOT TO GLORIFY BUT, ONLY TO IDENTIFY THOSE
SITUATIONS IN THE HOODZ.

(SONG – JESUS IS LOVE)

THE CROWD "GOD said it! Jesus will fix it, thaz wha GOD said, and I believe it!"

Then Miss H. begin to say the words and the crowd would say again.

THE CROWD "I believe it!"

As if she was telling a story. Miss H. began saying.

MISS H "Jesus went to the mountain just to pray."

Crowd said.

CROWD "I believe it!"

Miss H. said.

MISS H "He is the same then and the same today!"

NOT TO GLORIFY BUT, ONLY TO IDENTIFY THOSE SITUATIONS IN THE HOODZ.

Crowd said.

CROWD "I believe it!"

Miss H. said.

MISS H "wha GOD gives to you no one can take away!"

Crowd said.

CROWD "I believe it! I believe it!"

Master looks around with his sneaky smile as he gallops along on his white horse. A look of satisfaction with his power to control people with his whip. He began to laugh out loud as he cracks his whip down on their backs, and then he shouts.

PERVIS "Shut up! Get movin! Hurry up!"

Then he looks over to the overseer and shakes his head up and down as he continued to smile. As they get to the field the slaves file off into

single lines and they begin their work; picking
cotton.

Miss H. begin to pick her cotton, as she looks up
at the sun that begin to rise, she sees the sun
rays as it begins to cover the field with its
radiant light, then it raised above the field and
hills.

Miss H. looked around at the people and began
to smile at them as some peeped over at her
trying to figure out what she was smiling about.
No one saw what Miss H. saw, and what she saw
was a sun lit field with her people shining in the
mist of all the negative energy that surround
them.

This gave her hope once again that GOD is the
good news for them to pray about, and believe
in. Then the sweat begins to roll down her
brow, she saw one of the elderly ladies of the
crowd begin to sway back and forth like she
was going to faint.

Miss H. heart just melted with sorrow, and then

she began to sing.

MISS H "There is Victory in Jesus, hallelujah; there is victory in Jesus, hallelujah; there is victory in Jesus, hallelujah; Victory in Jesus, hallelujah!"

The whole field was in harmony, on one accord focused on Jesus. The elderly lady who looked like she was about to faint turned around and looked over at Miss H. and smiled with amazement of what Miss H. had just done, which was to give hope once again to the people who failed in strength for that moment.

Master PERVIS speaking to the overseer as he points his hand over the field with a satisfied smile.

PERVIS "You see how they work when she's around; as long as I keep her in her place they'll work like that forever. They look happy, don't they?"

Master PERVIS and the overseer laughed

together as if to know what the singing was all
about.

(ABOUT A MONTH LATER)

**Miss H. has been tormented long enough! That
morning as Master PERVIS and the overseer
begin to round up the slaves from their shacks.
Master PERVIS was at Miss H. door and burst
in. Miss H. said once again.**

**MISS H "Master PERVIS sir, I'm sorry
sir!"**

**As she jumps up from her knees from praying
as Master PERVIS stands at her door after
kicking it in. She runs by him to file in line as
the crowd waits for her outside. Master
PERVIS shouts.**

PERVIS "Sorry, sorry!"

**As he raises his whip over her head to draw
blood. Just then a young slave named Sam steps
in front of her to take the whipping. "CRACK!"**

"SWOOSH!" "CRACK!" Went the whip across Sam's back. As Master PERVIS spills blood from Sam's back, then he yells.

PERVIS "Thaz right, come on in, join us, we gonna have a party!"

Sam just looks at Master PERVIS with a stern look as if to say; (drop the whip, now!) Then Master PERVIS takes a good look at Sam's back before it's covered with blood and he takes a step back from Sam and calls over to the overseer.

PERVIS "Head 'em up, move 'em out!"

Then Master PERVIS cracks his whip once again across Sam's back as he gets on his white horse. As they begin to march to the fields Miss H. grab Sam's hand while they march and she sings in a low voice.

MISS H "My head may be filled with water, mine eyes a fountain of tears, I may weep day and night but, my lord calms all my fears.

NOT TO GLORIFY BUT, ONLY TO IDENTIFY THOSE SITUATIONS IN THE HOODZ.

Hallelujah, thank you Lord, Hallelujah, praise his name, Hallelujah, thank you Lord, Hallelujah, praise his name!"

As the crowd march on they join in as she begins to hum and sing.

Miss H "Jesus, my head may be filled with water, Jesus, mine eyes a fountain of tears. Jesus, I may weep day and night, thank you Jesus, you calm all of my fears; Hallelujah, Jesus, we love you Lord!"

As a whip echoes in the background a scream is heard faintly. They file off into a single file and begin their chores; they begin picking cotton as if nothing has happened.

(THAT NIGHT BEHIND THE BIG SHACK WHERE MANY GATHERED UNDER ONE ROOF. "THE SHADOW OF THE MOON")

As the crowd warmed themselves by the fire, someone took a stick and waved at the fire, as if they were fussing it out. (Cursing it out) As the flames grew taller the crowd backed up.

Then others reached out their hands for a chance to fuss at the flames. Then it began. Miss H. begins to hum, and then, someone handed her the stick she grabbed it with both hands one on each end.

She lifted it over her head then she turned around and took a step close to the fire then took a step back. Then as she broke away from the fire, (still with stick in hand) the crowd begins to sing:

CROWD "Yah-A-Yah, Yami-Yami, Yah-A-Yah, thank you Lord! Yah-A-Yah, Yami-Yami, Yah-A-Yah, thank you Lord! Yah-A-Yah, Yami-Yami, Yah-Yah, thank you Lord!"

She begins to sway back and forth as if the stick was guiding her. Then she stepped side to side turning around held the stick out to pass it to another person. They too, stepped to the fire, then backed up, lift the stick over their head.

NOT TO GLORIFY BUT, ONLY TO IDENTIFY THOSE
SITUATIONS IN THE HOODZ.

Stepped close to the fire swayed from side to
side then past the stick. On and on it went till
they were satisfied that the fire was under
control, flames all at one level; not raising or
lowering, calm as water.

When their granddaddy described this part of
their history Jackee began to cry. The tears
streamed down her cheeks. She started to sway
back and forth stretching out her hands with
her eyes closed.

Then Grandmomma pointed over to Jackee and
granddaddy   smiled   and   nodded   in
acknowledgement of the spirit which filled the
room as he told about their past. Then
granddaddy started up again. Granddaddy
whispers that Miss H. sings as the crowd moved
to her song.

MISS H "Neither is their salvation in any
other. He is Lord of all! Build us up a nation,
send us a mother. He is Lord of all! Strength
and courage, we stand tall like we should. He is
Lord of all! Jesus he is Lord of all! Jesus, he is

Lord of all! Jesus, he is Lord of all!"

As the stick is passed, the crowd lift up their hands and their heads to the sky, then they all drop to the ground on bent knees saying.

CROWD "He is Lord of all!"

The young man Sam arose, looked at Miss H. held out his hand and said.

SAM "Be it known unto you all, and to the people of this plantation, that by the name of Jesus Christ whom was crucified, whom GOD raised from the dead; by him do we stand here before you whole heartedly in prayer Miss H!"

Someone jumped up saying,

SOMEONE "Hallelujah!"

Another jumped up saying,

ANOTHER "Praise the Lord!"

NOT TO GLORIFY BUT, ONLY TO IDENTIFY THOSE SITUATIONS IN THE HOODZ.

Then everyone got up praising his name.

EVERYONE "JESUS, JESUS!"

And the Holly Ghost fell upon them as they went back to their shacks for the night singing and praising GOD.

(LATER THAT YEAR SOMETHING STRANGE HAPPENED TO THE ONE CALLED CHARLES THAT WOULD CHANGE HIS LIFE FOREVER.)

"Knock, Knock!" On miss H door.

SOMEONE SHOUTED "Miss H. you in there? Wake up!"

Someone shouted again.

SOMEONE "The water Miss H, the water!"

They knocked again. "Knock, Knock, Knock!"

Miss H. arose and went to the door, opened it

and saw Charles a young thin tall boy with hands reaching out for Miss H. waving to her to come on. As the others gathered in the moonlight. The crowd of people was increasing.

Charles said.

CHARLES "He's been good to me, yes he has, he's been good to me. Hallelujah!"

Then Charles waved her to come on once again as he says.

CHARLES "Take me to the water Miss H."

And he sings as he waves her on and walks toward the water.

MISS H "Down by the river, the water flows, it starts out small but then it grows, in Jesus name, take me to the water, I have no shame."

Miss H. shaking her head no, as she sings.

MISS H "None but the righteous, none but

the righteous to be baptized."

Everyone in the background starts feeling the spirit and start singing. As the slow march begins and they begin to step to the song, dust began to rise from the stepping and they begin to look like they were on a cloud of mist.

Miss H. said with a smile.

   Miss H "Take him to the water; take him to the water, to be baptized."

As she shakes her head and points a finger at him with one hand on her hip she says.

   MISS H "Don't be playin with your heart, boy!"

Charles is filled with the Holy Ghost, Miss H. grabs his hand and leads him to the fish pond beyond the fields just on the other side. Where he is to be dipped into the water, as she blesses him of the father, the son and the Holy Spirit.

Miss H. speaks as she wades through the water and climb on top of a giant rock in the middle of the pond.

MISS H "This rock represents the place of baptism for all who believe, and for you Charles who claim to believe.

As she stretches out her arms above her head.

MISS H "We shall see your faith in which you proclaim to have!"

The crowd that stood on the land stomp their right foot then the left foot. As the left foot came down the men with the heavy voices whispered.

CROWD "HUUH! SHA-LOAM!"

Miss H. then said.

MISS H "A wise man will build his house on a rock and when the rains come and the winds blow and beat on the house it will not fall!"

NOT TO GLORIFY BUT, ONLY TO IDENTIFY THOSE
SITUATIONS IN THE HOODZ.

Charles said.

CHARLES "My faith will stand firm!"

Miss H then said.

MISS H "For it was founded on the rock of
salvation, and Charles this should mean to you.

As she lowered her hands and look down at
Charles standing at the bottom of the rock
looking up.

MISS H "The foundation of your faith
should be built upon a rock in order to stand
strong for the Lord."

And the crowd on land said as they stomped.

CROWD "HUUH! SHA-LOAM! A-A-A-A

Then they stomped.

CROWD "HUUH! SHA-LOAM! A-A-A-A

NOT TO GLORIFY BUT, ONLY TO IDENTIFY THOSE SITUATIONS IN THE HOODZ.

(STOMP)

Then Miss H. said.

MISS H "My book tells me that a church shall be upon a rock and the gates of hell shall not prevail against it!"

Charles lifts up his hands and spoke unto the sky

CHARLES "Here I am Lord, use me father, and come upon me this day with your HOLY GHOST power!"

Then Miss H. said.

MISS H "I will call upon the Lord, who is worthy to be praised; My GOD, my GOD, and my strength in whom I will trust!"

Then the crowd shouted out with loud voices of joy. The crowd of people sang.

CROWD "YAH-A-YAH, (stomp) HUUH!

NOT TO GLORIFY BUT, ONLY TO IDENTIFY THOSE
SITUATIONS IN THE HOODZ.

HUUH! SHA-LOAM! A-A-A-A!"

As the tenors, bass, sopranos, all the voices
came together with a stomp beat, the cloud of
dust appeared around the pond and begin to
rise.

(MEANWHILE)

Grandmomma pointed out from the side to
show granddaddy that Mikee and CeCe had
their eyes closed and the spirit joined in, as
their room was filled with the Holy Ghost of the
past, present, and future.

Granddaddy acknowledged her with a nod of
the head as he continued to tell of who they are
and who's they are.

(STORY)

As Miss H. looked down from the rock at
Charles and spoke, Charles made eye contact
with her as she waved her hands over his head
and she said.

NOT TO GLORIFY BUT, ONLY TO IDENTIFY THOSE
SITUATIONS IN THE HOODZ.

MISS H "Bless those who curse you, do good
to those who hate you, pray for those who
spitefully use you and persecute you!"

Then Miss H. lifts up her hands to the sky and
said.

MISS H "Only by GOD's grace have you
been saved!"

She stepped down from the rock and laid one
hand on Charles forehead and the other she lifts
to the sky. Two elderly men were walking
toward them as she took her hand from his
forehead and dipped it into the water.

The two elders held Charles arms and rubbed
his back as she put her hand back on his
forehead and said.

MISS H "I baptize thee in the FATHER,
THE SON, and THE HOLY GHOST!"

Then the two elderly men dipped Charles in the

water, as the singing and stomping continued.
Charles rose up from the water. Miss H begins
to sing.

MISS H "Walkin through the valley, the
shadow of death, fearin no evil, thou art with
me, thy rod and the staff, shall comfort me, thy
filleth my cup, my cup runneth over, goodness
and mercy, shall follow me."

As the elders walk with Charles through the
water to be greeted by the crowd singing and
dancing Charles turned and looked at Miss H.
and begin to sing with her in a loud voice.

There was singing and dancing as Charles put
on a blanket and headed for his dwelling place.
As months went by Charles grew strong in the
Lord as a teacher to the young children.

(LATER THAT YEAR)

Late one night there was shouting and
screaming around Miss H. shack. A young girl
named Issy was shouting.

NOT TO GLORIFY BUT, ONLY TO IDENTIFY THOSE SITUATIONS IN THE HOODZ.

ISSY "Come quickly, Miss H.!"

Then a knock came at her door. "KNOCK, KNOCK!"

Miss H. finally got up as she dragged herself to the door. Issy said.

ISSY "Miss H., Miss H.! Open the door!"

As Miss H. open the door Issy came right pass her then turned around and started to say something but Miss H. said something first.

MISS H "Good morning, and Praise the Lord to you too."

Then Issy said.

ISSY "Oh yeah, good morning Miss H."

As the sweat poured off her brow, it looked like someone poured water down her face.

NOT TO GLORIFY BUT, ONLY TO IDENTIFY THOSE SITUATIONS IN THE HOODZ.

MISS H "Whaz goin on? Whaz wrong Issy?"

Issy said.

ISSY "Master PERVIS, its Master PERVIS, he's hurt, thrown from his horse early this morning."

Miss H. shaking her head back and forth as she went to grab her shawl to put around her along with her bible.

Miss H said with an attitude.

MISS H "I bet he'd been drinkin again."

She said to Issy as she shook her head and mumbling, Issy started pacing the floor and finally answered.

ISSY "Yes sum, he was drunken ma'am."

MISS H "Well how bad is he this time?"

Issy said, "His shoulder or neck ma'am, it's

hard to tell with him cussin and fussin and all.
No one can touch him to see."

As Miss H. and Issy entered into the field area
where Master PERVIS laid, they could hear
him whooping and hollering in pain as people
around him tried to help.

Master PERVIS says as he tries to get up off the
ground.

PERVIS "Ooh, ahh, ooh, ahh, back up off
me you little cotton pickers, hands off me, you
pickenninnies! Where's my horse? Ooh, ahh."

As the tears rolled down his cheek, the crowd
opened up as the overseer came up the road.

Overseer said.

OVERSEER "You'll lookin for a whuppin?
Move, move, get out the way!"

He shoved his way to master PERVIS, he
leaned over master PERVIS, looked at the

blood and vomit, with him lying in his own urine. The overseer reached out to grab him but, the urine smell entered his nose.

He gasped for air to pick up master PERVIS he made a funny look on his face. Then just when he had a grip on master PERVIS arm they both fell to the ground. Master PERVIS screamed for mercy.

PERVIS "Help me Lord! Help me Lord!"

As he clawed his way off of the overseer, trying to stand up his eyes opened up and Miss H. appeared. Miss H. said with pleasure.

MISS H "Say it, gone say it, come on let me hear it!"

She bent down to touch his shoulder, then his neck he screamed. Just as the overseer got into position with his whip to strike her, Sam stepped from out the crowd and walked toward the overseer.

NOT TO GLORIFY BUT, ONLY TO IDENTIFY THOSE SITUATIONS IN THE HOODZ.

(MASTER PERVIS THEN PASSED OUT.)

(SONG – ROCK MY SOUL)

Sam said.

    SAM "How issum Miss H.?"

She looked up and stared at the overseer as he slowly put his whip down.

Sam said.

    SAM "Issum gonna make it?"

Sam asking Miss H., and not once did he take his eyes off the overseer. The overseer backed up one step as Sam stepped forward toward Miss H. Then she stood up between Sam and the Overseer.

    MISS H "Yes Sam, hims okay."

She said with a smile. Then she glazed into

Sam's eyes, and there was a sparkle for one second and Miss H. saw it. (Then she took one step back in amazement of the sparkle she saw in his eyes.) As she turned to the overseer and looked him square in the face she said.

MISS H "Help me take him to the big house Sam."

Then the overseer and Sam both lift him up and carried him to the big house. Then some of the crowd went to their shack others followed to the big house. Miss H. opened her raggedy bible book, read some words and prayed out loud as she laid hands on Master PERVIS.

Miss H. said.

MISS H "In the name of JESUS heal this old body Lord, help this brother to be strong once again. Help him oh Lord to walk again, and Jesus I want you to heal him from pain, that's right Lord take his pain away and then Lord heal his mind Lord, so he can think straight."

NOT TO GLORIFY BUT, ONLY TO IDENTIFY THOSE
SITUATIONS IN THE HOODZ.

Just then Master PERVIS reached out grabbed her hand pushed it off him and said in a wild and crazy voice.

PERVIS "Wha-chu means heal my mind girl! Who-chu think you talkin too! Don't chu know?" (Ooh, ooh, ahhh, ahhh.)

Then Master PERVIS passed out again, as Sam looked at Miss H. and smiled the crowd behind them start shouting "AMEN" to the preaching she was doing, especially about healing the mind part.

The crowd stopped at the steps of the big house, as Sam looked at Miss H. the overseer motioned him to come on, go in. It was the first time Sam ever been inside the big house. Sam looked up at the ceiling then he looked down at the floor.

Then at the table with wooden dishes, spoons, and forks cleaned. Then the overseer motioned Sam to follow him upstairs. As the bedroom door opened Sam almost dropped Master PERVIS when he saw the inside of the room.

The bed was huge that master PERVIS was put
on. Then Miss H. prayed again for healing, as
she massaged master PERVIS neck, she looked
up at the house lady and the houseman (cook
and butler slave) then she called out orders for
everyone.

MISS H "I need onions, hot water, horse
radish, for fever and muscle healin also garlic
and clean rags too! Now get goin, hurry,
hurry!"

As she waved one hand in the air for them to go.
Other house servants ran to get those things
that she needed. Then Miss H. held out her
hand for Sam's hand and Sam held out his
hand for the overseer's other hand.

Then they circled around master PERVIS, she
prayed again for master PERVIS healing and
wellbeing. Just then Master PERVIS eyes
opened up and he screamed.

PERVIS "Wha-chu think, that I'm dead or

sum-ump! You betta get back to work, this ain't no day off! Get I say, get!"

As the overseer and Sam begin to leave the room the house servants came rushing through the doorway with what Miss H. had asked for. Sam left the room he looked over his shoulder and made eye contact with Miss H. and they smiled at each other.

Miss H. recognized Sam smile of surrender unto her peacefulness and she blushed.

Then the overseer said.

OVERSEER "Come on Sam, come on."

After that day Sam and Miss H. walked together, talked together, and prayed together. Before you knew it they were soon to be married.

(JUMP THE BROOMSTICK)

3 days before the marriage were the exciting

days everyone on the plantation watched and enjoyed. During the 3 days each day Miss H. and Sam performed different LOVE HONORS.

The first day she would clean his shack; the way a man keeps his shack would let the women know how clean he is. The second day when they saw each other they would have to dance every time they looked at each other.

Depending on the joy in their hearts about their future marriage would determine how strong and graceful their dance would be. On the third day they would pray all day together at a distance never stopping. He looks at her, she would pray.

She looks at him he would pray all day long back and forth on and on. To not clean house, cook, dance, or pray with one another would mean their heart was not on one accord and they could break it off (the wedding) at any time.

Everybody was excited they all watched each

day for three days. It was funny and serious all at the same time. The kids all loved to see the dance because no matter how tired each of them was (man or woman).

Whenever they looked at each other far off at a distance, they could see one of them dance on one side of the field, and the other on the other side of the field. People laughed as they looked from side to side each dancing after the other stop.

Everyone peeped up from his or her work to watch the dancing and working Sam and Miss H. would perform that day. (And it was a funny sight.) Miss H. dance in the fields. (2 left feet; stomp, stomp, 2 right feet; stomp, stomp, then 2 jumps and head snap back and forth.)

Then across the field Sam danced the same. They both look like two roosters who were ready to fight, and a rabbit that jump from bush to bush hiding from the giant birds. All day long they just couldn't keep their eyes off one another.

That's what signaled other people of how strong
their LOVE is. If they danced a little that means
a little love was there if they danced a lot, a lot
of love was there; and they danced a lot.

Cooking was another ritual, when she cooked
for him it was a wholesome meal full with gravy
and biscuits and meat. Sam didn't cook dinner
to well for Miss H. the meat was too tough and
her biscuits were hard.

But, Sam made her breakfast very well and
Miss H. knew she had to work on Sam's dinner
with him. When the last day came and they
prayed, it looked like each of them was going
out of their minds.

Talking to the Lord smiling at the air, they both
were filled with the spirit, the Holy Ghost
Spirit. If their praying was not out of joy the
people would sense the lack of love for one
another.

If there were no smiles, the people would know

that this marriage would not be a true marriage and the elders of the plantation would be watching closely to detect or scrutinize the sincerity of each expression of prayer.

The day finally came and the fields were filled with joy, no matter how hard the overseer worked Sam and Miss H. they both smiled and kept going. Then Master PERVIS called Sam and Miss H. out of the field and with both of them at one time in front of him.

He said in a low voice, as he looked them up and down while making a snarling sound. (as if he were better than them).

PERVIS "So, you think I don't know whaz goin on huh? Well, I tell you, nothing goes on round here wit out me knowin, you hear me boy!"

As he looks at Sam, eye to eye then steps over to Miss H. and say.

PERVIS "I bet I can get a pretty penny for a

strong spiritual little boy. You make sure it be a boy, you hear me Miss H.! A baby boy?"

As he stepped back to see Sam's reaction putting one hand on his whip at his side when he sensed Miss H. mocking him with her expression of yes sir, with a smile. Then Sam spoke up.

SAM "Wha if it's a baby girl sir? Huh sir?"

Master PERVIS relaxed his arm and shouted.

PERVIS "Then you keep tryin till you gets me a boy, now ya'll get back to the fields and don't forget; I'm watchin ya!"

Sam said with a smile.

SAM "Yes sum, we know dat you watchin sir, we's be careful sir, so we's can get-chu tha boy sir."

Miss H. said along with Sam.

NOT TO GLORIFY BUT, ONLY TO IDENTIFY THOSE SITUATIONS IN THE HOODZ.

MISS H AND SAM "Yes sum sir, we gonna get-chu tha boy sir, you wait and see sir."

Then Master **PERVIS** smiled with satisfaction and said.

PERVIS "Thaz right ya'll have a real good marriage, hear me, now get! Stop wastin my time, get!"

As Sam and Miss H. walked back to the field, they laughed and giggled and smiled at each other holding hands. Then the overseer directed Sam to his part of the field and Miss H. to her part of the field. That night was the celebration of jumping the broomstick.

The reason they used the broomstick was because it symbolized, and represented the straight way they would take from that day forth. Never to detour from one another always abiding in each other's strength.

Knowing the fastest route to the heart is a straight route not a curve. With that knowledge

they would deal with problems straight through
and not round about.

(THAT NIGHT)

As people begin to gather under the moon lit
sky, the air was filled with the smell of cooked
meat, collard greens and potatoes. There was
soon to be a party/celebration this wedding
night. The elders of the plantation (one man
and one woman) held the stick high above the
ground about waste high as the crowd hummed
one of Miss H. prayer hymns.

They opened up the middle of the crowd as
Miss H. and Sam came walking side by side
holding hands. They strolled gracefully
together, stepping left foot, and right foot
together looking as proud as peacocks on a
matting call strutting with chest puffed out.

Miss H. had a turban wrapped around her head
with her shawl draped on one side hanging
around her body. One piece, her dress dragged
the ground behind her, the children followed,

NOT TO GLORIFY BUT, ONLY TO IDENTIFY THOSE
SITUATIONS IN THE HOODZ.

then young adults and then grownups (men and women).

With children first, celebrates the innocence of this marriage in the beginning, and how it shall grow to the end with the elders representing the end. Sam had a black scarf wrapped around his head and tied in the back.

The end pieces hung down like a raccoon tail hat, his shirt hung outside his pants (long like a jacket). He also had a black scarf wrapped around his waist to match the scarf wrapped around his head and it hung down on his right side.

Her turban and shawl was black and her dress was a golden brown and his shirt and pants were light brown. As the broomstick was placed on the ground just before they got in front of it, Sam looked at Miss H. with a big old smile.

Just then Miss H. saw that sparkle in his eye once again and begin to cry as they both jumped at the same time. As they both leaped in

the air they turned toward each other and
landed on their feet facing each other.

As the crowd cheered them on they begin to kiss
and hug each other with great joy. The whole
time there were no words being said to disrupt
the Holy Spirit before they jumped. There was
a big celebration that night around the
plantation and a lot of dancing and food.

Once and a while Sam would look up at the big
house and he could see one light on in the
second floor bedroom window where they all
knew Master PERVIS slept. Sam knew that he
was watching their every move.

Then his wife came and hugged him as he
stared up at the house he felt a sign of relief as
she kissed his cheek to let him know that GOD
is in control.

(MEANWHILE AS GRANDDADDY TOLD
THE STORY)

Granddaddy looked over at Grandmomma and

NOT TO GLORIFY BUT, ONLY TO IDENTIFY THOSE
SITUATIONS IN THE HOODZ.

they both smiled as they saw all three kids with their eyes closed, meditating on the last of his words. Granddaddy finally said.

GRANDDADDY "And now kids, you finally know WHO YOU ARE, AND WHO'S YOU ARE!

It's time for bed and don't forget that you cab comes at eight o'clock in the morning. No one moved their eyes were shut tight but, Grandmomma knew what to do and she said in a loud voice.

GRANDMOMMA "What, yawl need hearin aids? You heard your granddaddy!"

They all jumped up and ran to their granddaddy and hugged him and then to their Grandmomma and gave her a hug and went off to bed with tears in their eyes. The next morning the cab came, they kissed, hugged, and cried.

Then they drove off waving goodbye heading

back to the city to their Momma-Tanya arms. As the cab pulled up to the house CeCe was the first to open her eyes, she pushed Mikee, and Mikee pushed Jackee and they saw Momma-Tanya.

Along with Tammy, Saraj, Brenda, Jim, Kent, and Jojo waiting on the front porch. When they got out the cab it was like a family reunion, everybody talking about everything all at once as they grabbed bags and food and luggage and walked in the house.

They all sat down in the living room and talked about their summer vacation. As Jackee was explaining about their spiritual awakening CeCe blurted out.

CECE "Hey, wait a minute, what about the talent show?"

Mikee said nonchalantly.

MIKEE "Baptism is 5pm; the talent show is a 7:30pm. All we have to do is take one thing at a time."

Momma-Tanya looked over at Mikee and said.

MOMMA-TANYA "Michael is that you I hear? So you did learn something at Grandmomma and granddaddy's house."

They all laughed at the way Mikee took his time and explained the situation to them, because he usually run all his sentences together while rushing his thoughts.

Jackee said.

JACKEE "So, the whole time I was talkin to you at night (looking over at Brenda) you mean to tell me that you start goin to church?"

Tammy said.

TAMMY "Well, the way you said how the Holy Spirit had touched your heart. We just had to see wha-chu was talkin bout."

NOT TO GLORIFY BUT, ONLY TO IDENTIFY THOSE
SITUATIONS IN THE HOODZ.

As they begin to laugh, Momma-Tanya said in a
shocking voice.

MOMMA-TANYA "You mean to tell me
that, all you kids been going to church this
summer, even you boys?"

All the kids said with great pride and sincerity.

ALL THE KIDS "Yes ma'am."

They all laughed and got up and gave each
other a high five. It looked like they were
having a party and they begin to step to a beat.
CeCe looked at her mother and grabbed her
arm ushering her to get up as CeCe sang.

CECE "Party, come on momma, party."

(As they stepped and clapped their hands to the
beat.)

Mikee said.

MIKEE "Ain't no party like the HOLY

NOT TO GLORIFY BUT, ONLY TO IDENTIFY THOSE SITUATIONS IN THE HOODZ.

GHOST party, cause the HOLT GHOST party is the BOMB!"

They all joined in with Mikee and begin to step. (Even Momma-Tanya) and it sounded like a party up in the house.

(5pm AT CHRUCH)

The preacher said.

PREACHER "There's a witness out there somewhere who can testify. Stand up, that's right, stand up, and be a witness of GOD's goodness and mercy."

Baptism was just finished and the preacher was about to close church with a prayer and all of a sudden the HOLY GHOST SPIRIT filled the church. Out of the crowd of people who stood up was Jojo, Kent, and Mikee begin to sing in harmony.

This sounded like a harmony prayer as Percy, Jim and two other guys were changing out of their white robes from being baptized.

Kent said out loud.

KENT "Jeesus!"

Jojo said right behind him.

JOJO "Jeesus!"

Then they sat down together and then sung in a low voice.

KENT AND JOJO "I LOVE you Lord, I LOVE you LOORD, I LOVE YOU JEESUS!"

Then Kent stood up again singing.

KENT "YOU ARE MY STRENGTH."

Then Jojo stood up again singing.

JOJO "YOU DIED FOR ME AT CALVERY."

NOT TO GLORIFY BUT, ONLY TO IDENTIFY THOSE
SITUATIONS IN THE HOODZ.

Then Mikee stood up singing.

MIKEE "You picked me up when I was down."

The preacher was so happy that he shouted.

PREACHER "Can we get an AMEN: now we got time for one more."

Jim stood up and he looked over his shoulder at Mr. Kake, and Miss Brewster. Mr. Kake just sat there with a big smile on his face as if something wonderful was about to happen.

Jim said.

JIM "At first I thought you had to be a chump, or a sissy to sit down and listen to a preacher, to come to church, to praise the Lord. Then I came to the shelter and realized that, I'm a young proud teenager. I can stand up straight, walk with the Lord and be proud to walk in his light because of who I am, cause I choose too!"

NOT TO GLORIFY BUT, ONLY TO IDENTIFY THOSE SITUATIONS IN THE HOODZ.

Jackee stood up with her hands in the air shouting and begins to dance. CeCe pulled her by the arm to sit her down; she looked around as if to be embarrassed and sat down.

Jackee finally said.

JACKEE "Hallelujah, Hallelujah, thank you JESUS!"

Then Jim finished up by saying.

JIM "For him to die for my sins, for him to heal the sick, for him to raise up from the dead and walk again, and still forgive people."

(Then from out of nowhere Percy jumped up and shouted.)

PERCY "And for him to save a wretch like me!"

Jim said.

NOT TO GLORIFY BUT, ONLY TO IDENTIFY THOSE SITUATIONS IN THE HOODZ.

JIM "I've got too!"

Then Percy said again.

PERCY "I've got too!"

Then Brenda shouted as she stood up.

BRENDA "I've got too!"

Then Saraj stood up and shouted.

SARAJ "I've got too!"

Jim finally said.

JIM "GIVE GOD THE GLORY!"

As the tears flowed from Jim face he stomped his feet with extreme gratefulness, threw his hands up in the air and shouted.

JIM "HALLELUJAH, HALLELUJAH!"

Then CeCe stood up and started to clap. Then

she begins to sing the words from Psalms 23:4
that her great, great, great grandma Miss H.,
sang back in the day.

CECE "Walkin through the valley, the
shadow of death, fearin no evil, thou art with
me, thy rod and thy staff, shall com-fort me, thy
filleth my cup, my cup runneth over. Goodness
and mercy, shall fol-low me, asss, I walk
through the valley;"

Then she repeated it over again. They all sang
and stepped as they left the church. It was a
Holy Night with a Beautiful Sight of Babies
Being Born of the SPIRIT. Jackee, Mikee,
CeCe, Brenda, Kent, Jojo, Jim, Percy, Saraj,
and Tammy, then had to call a cab because the
whole crew had to rush over to the school for
the talent show.

(AS SARAJ COMPLAINED ABOUT HOW
CROWDED THE CAB IS)

Jackee said. "Pass out those papers Mikee,
and read whaz on it, cause everybody's name is

at the top."

As Mikee passed out the papers Jackee then said.

JACKEE "Look ya'll, we'll be the last act to go on stage so, everybody in the audience will be tired. It will be our job to M.C."

Then CeCe raised her hand, and so did Saraj. Brenda said.

CECE "What about the music, did you bring it, and whaz M.C. Jackee?"

Mikee Said.

MIKEE "Move the crowd, little sis."

Saraj said.

SARAJ "I can't memorize all these lines."

Jackee said.

NOT TO GLORIFY BUT, ONLY TO IDENTIFY THOSE
SITUATIONS IN THE HOODZ.

JACKEE "Naw, Saraj and Brenda we gonna take these papers on stage and read, act, sing, and step with an ATTITUDE! I've got the music, we just sing to the beat and step with an attitude ok, and the crowd will catch on to the beat and we'll be alright."

Jojo said.

JOJO "Now thaz my kind of actin!"

As he read the paper Mikee handed to him.

Brenda said.

BRENDA "From what I'm readin so far it sounds like a serious gospel comedy."

Jackee said.

JACKEE "You got it my sista now, everybody start readin their part. We have a half hour before we go on stage."

Percy said.

PERCY "I sure hope this bum turns out to
be a good guy cause I've been a bad guy all my
life and it kinda gets old after you clean up your
act. You know what I mean?"

Jackee and Jim smiled at each other.

Tammy said.

TAMMY "Don't worry my brutha we gonna
be steppin so hard and so serious that you'll
look good even when you look bad."

They all laughed and Jackee said.

JACKEE "This all came to me from the
book of Matthew chap. 7, verse 1 and 2. THOU
SHALL NOT JUDGE!"

Kent said.

KENT "Now thaz what I'm talkin bout! So,
wha-up with the steppin?"

NOT TO GLORIFY BUT, ONLY TO IDENTIFY THOSE SITUATIONS IN THE HOODZ.

Jackee said.

JACKEE "Remember all those step team steps you use to watch me do? Well, welcome to our new step team."

They all laughed once again.

Jim said.

(SONG – BATTLEFIELD)

JIM "Yeah, once upon a time I would have left you standin here my sista but, today I'm a proud young Christian Brutha and I feel like I'm in GOD'S ARMY NOW!"

Kent and Jojo hollered.

KENT AND JOJO "Praise the Lord! Let's get it on, let's do it!"

Jackee smiled and said.

JACKEE "We have just enough time for me

NOT TO GLORIFY BUT, ONLY TO IDENTIFY THOSE SITUATIONS IN THE HOODZ.

to read the synopsis to you and then it's on!"

They all cheered.

THEY CHEERED "Praise the Lord, let's do it!"

As she read the synopsis of the scene in which they were to take the step and song from.

(THE BUM WALKED BY 3 KIDS ON THE BLOCK AND TRIES TO TALK TO THEM)

No. #1 kid.

#1 KID "Hey man watch where you goin! Get off my block!"

Bum said.

BUM "On my block kids are sellin dope!"

No. #1 kid.

#1 KID "Man, we not sellin dope, we be

sellin smack and crack; and you keep talkin we gonna attack your sorry butt!"

Bum asked.

BUM "How old are you, young dope dealer?"

(AS HE STEPS TO ANOTHER KID)

No. #2 kid.

#2 KID "I'm 11, he's 12, and he's 13; keep it up and we gonna show you just how mean we can be!"

Bum says as he walks past the 2nd kid;

BUM "Some say your manhood will never be seen!"

No. #3 kid said.

#3 KID "Wha-chu know about manhood, you just a bum!"

NOT TO GLORIFY BUT, ONLY TO IDENTIFY THOSE SITUATIONS IN THE HOODZ.

Bum said.

BUM "Am I crazy, or are you just plain lazy? He worked hard all day!"

No. #1 kid said.

#1 KID "Wha-chu mean lazy, we're out here every day, and we get paid!"

(THEN 2 YOUNG GIRLS WALKED UP AND START HUGGING 2 OF THE KIDS.)

Bum said.

BUM "You'll leave your young girlfriends with a habit or baby."

No. #1 kid said.

#1 KID "Man, watch your mouth before I bust a cap in you! Talkin bout our girls like that."

NOT TO GLORIFY BUT, ONLY TO IDENTIFY THOSE
SITUATIONS IN THE HOODZ.

No. #1 Girl said.

#1 GIRL "Yeah, I don't know who he thinks
he is, talkin to me like that!"

No. #2 Girl said.

#2 GIRL "Hold up, I kick his butt!"

(As she put up her dukes with an attitude.)

Bum said.

BUM "Dare to be free like me; to be behind
bars is just plain crazy! Look at the old man
blisters!"

(As he holds out both hands for them to look
at.)

No. #1 kid; said.

#1 KID "Anyone wants to be a bum, raise
your hand?"

NOT TO GLORIFY BUT, ONLY TO IDENTIFY THOSE
SITUATIONS IN THE HOODZ.

As they all laughed when he opens his coat to
show his bible he said.

BUM "I rebuke you in the name of JESUS!
And, they shall flee from thee. Don't let them
take you in tight!"

No. #2 kid said.

#2 KID "Thaz it, keep walkin or else!"

Then he reaches in his dip to pull out his
rodscoe (gun).

No. #1 kid said.

#1 KID "Naw, I'm not gonna let you waste
your bullets on him. So keep walkin bum!"

No. #1 and 2 Girls say together.

#1 and 2 GIRL "yeah, keep walkin BUM!"

As the bum points to the young girls, he says.

NOT TO GLORIFY BUT, ONLY TO IDENTIFY THOSE
SITUATIONS IN THE HOODZ.

BUM "The girlfriend with the habit is left
behind, another dope fiend she will soon find!"

(THEN HE WALKS OUT OF SIGHT)

When the cab pulled up they all jumped out
and rushed inside the school. When the stage
manager saw them he ushered them to get
ready because they were next to go on stage.
Then the curtains came down and all those on
stage exit it and Jackee and the others were
waved at to go on.

Jackee rushed out on stage and she began to
wave her hands over her head and the rest of
the guys Jojo, Brenda, and all came behind her
as the music begin to play. She grabbed both
mics and handed one to Jim and the other to
CeCe.

Then she began to step to the beat. Saraj and
Jim looked at their papers and then at each
other shrugged their shoulders and went for it.
Jackee shouted.

NOT TO GLORIFY BUT, ONLY TO IDENTIFY THOSE
SITUATIONS IN THE HOODZ.

JACKEE "Brutha and Sistas!"

She pointed to Jim and he said in a deep voice.

JIM "REMEMBER"

Then she pointed to the others and they said.

OTHERS "The old man blisters."

Then she pointed to CeCe and Mikee, and they
sang in harmony.

CECE AND MIKE "Lift up your head, and
hold it up high, we need your love, in order to
survive."

The audience began to clap as Jim began to rap
and the rest of them followed Jackee as she
stepped to the beat. (On My Block) When the
song ended, the audience stood up and gave
them a standing ovation.

NOT TO GLORIFY BUT, ONLY TO IDENTIFY THOSE
SITUATIONS IN THE HOODZ.

Jackee, Jim, and the rest of the crew stood on stage and gave a bow to the crowd as they laughed with excitement of finishing up the play with a rap song and step. Momma-Tanya and the other kid's parents were there and just as happy as the kids on stage.

Knowing that GOD is in control of all this, the kids on stage sent out one big kiss. All the groups came out on stage together they all reached out with arms open wide and waved to the audience.

But, for Jim, Jackee and their crew, that to them would symbolize their ATTITUDE OF GRATITUDE FOR GOD'S LOVE. Mr. Kake and a young lady walked up to the crowd of kids with their parents, also Momma-Tanya was especially happy to see them all in harmony for a worthy cause.

Mr. Kake introduced the young lady as Miss Lanae and that she was a playwright producer. She asked who wrote the play and Jackee said.

NOT TO GLORIFY BUT, ONLY TO IDENTIFY THOSE
SITUATIONS IN THE HOODZ.

JACKEE "Me and Jim wrote it."

Jim said.

JIM "You know I didn't write that, you
did!"

Jackee said.

JACKEE "I got the idea from your stories."

Jim said.

JIM "But, you put it on paper."

Then Jackee stepped closer to Jim and
whispered with teeth grittin, along with a half-
smile and heavy breathing and her fist balled
up.

Jackee said.

JACKEE "Jim if it wasn't for your story
telling time with Mikee and CeCe I wouldn't
have written it down!"

NOT TO GLORIFY BUT, ONLY TO IDENTIFY THOSE
SITUATIONS IN THE HOODZ.

Jim said.

JIM "Ok, ok, we did it Miss Lanae!"

Miss Lanae said.

LANAE "Wow, I'm glad we got that cleared
up. How would you like to write a full play?
Continuing the bum and kids because that's a
positive concept with a twist to it and I think
you guys are on to something big."

Mr. Kake looked at Momma-Tanya and the
others, he smiled a big smile as CeCe and some
others asked.

CECE AND OTHERS "What about the
steppin?"

Miss Lanae said.

LANAE "I want to produce it all. The play,
the song, the stepping because I love it, the idea
of it all; I don't know how far we could go with

it, but, I promise you that we will go far."

Just then Momma-Tanya said.

MOMMA-TANYA "Excuse me Miss Lanae but are you Lady Lanae from the Lanae School of the Arts?"

Miss Lanae answered as she extended her hand to Momma-Tanya for a hand shake.

LANAE "Yes I am."

Momma-Tanya said.

MOMMA-TANYA "Forgive me but, I thought that you would be a lot older."

Mr. Kake butted in and said.

KAKE "Well, she would be but, it was her mother who started the school."

As Jackee, Jim, CeCe, Saraj, Mikee, Percy and the others were still jumping for joy.

NOT TO GLORIFY BUT, ONLY TO IDENTIFY THOSE
SITUATIONS IN THE HOODZ.

Miss Lanae said.

LANAE "Oh yeah, this is my cousin Mr.
Kake he told me that he had something for me
to see at this talent show."

Jojo said.

JOJO "Shhhh, Shhhh, everybody they are
announcing the winner. And the winner is, is;
Not us!"

CeCe shouted.

CECE "Oh no, oh no, that means Miss
Lanae is not going to promote our play. Oh no,
oh no!"

Miss Lanae said.

LANAE "Now, now, young lady. I didn't
come here for the winner, I came for the
potential of longevity on something different
from the ordinary. Cousin Kake said I'd find it

here and he was right."

Jackee said.

JACKEE "So, how many skits do we need?"

CeCe said.

CECE "Yeah, cause Jim only told us one or two (voice muffled) hmmmm, (as Jim put his hand over CeCe's mouth).

Then Jim said.

JIM "Of many bum stories. I think we have about 6 or 8 skits."

Miss Lanae said.

LANAE "That's perfect, just what I'm talking about. Here's my card call me soon, ok!"

Mr. Kake said.

NOT TO GLORIFY BUT, ONLY TO IDENTIFY THOSE
SITUATIONS IN THE HOODZ.

KAKE "See you soon cousin Lanae be careful, love ya."

(As they hugged each other good night)

Jim and Jackee and the crew went nuts, they begin to jump up and down screaming;

THE CREW "Hallelujah Amen, Hallelujah Amen!"

Mr. Kake said.

KAKE "Ok kids, there's your blessing, now go for it. They're calling your name up there on stage."

They all waved and shouted thanks to him as their names were called for second place winners. They were all over joyed. They walked up on stage then walked across it holding hands and taking a bow as they received their trophy.

(THE CROWD ROARED WITH CLAPPING AND WHISTLING FOR THEM)

NOT TO GLORIFY BUT, ONLY TO IDENTIFY THOSE
SITUATIONS IN THE HOODZ.

The End.

Bloodline of the Hoodzville Playground, where chains are broken. "If it ain't rough, it ain't us!"

They flip tha scrip from negative to positive because; "It's one thing to live it, another to survive it!"

A Cast of 60 Characters

Jim	Mrs. Webster
Country	Mr. Ross
Lander	Miss Alfiena
Lander's mom	Miss Judy
Mark	Robert
Jackee	(Miss Cheryl)
Mac	First guy
Mikee	(Other guy)
CeCe	Momma-Tanya
Joey	(Deep voice)
#1 Kid	Lesley

NOT TO GLORIFY BUT, ONLY TO IDENTIFY THOSE
SITUATIONS IN THE HOODZ.

#2 Kid
#3 Kid
Bum
(Kathy-Cat)
(Lady holla's)
Junky
Percy
(Crowd agree)
(Girls rappin)
Judge
Mrs. Margie
Mrs. Brewster
Mr. Kake
Mr. Jefferies
(Class shouts)
Brenda
Tammy
JoJo
Kent
Saraj
(Guys shout)

Terry
Granddaddy
Grandmomma

Master PERVIS
 Miss H (Hazel)
 (Crowd)
 (Someone)
 (Another)
 (Everyone)
 Charles
  Issy
 Overseer
  Sam
 Preacher
#1 Girl
#2 Girl
 Mrs. Lanae

NOT TO GLORIFY BUT, ONLY TO IDENTIFY THOSE SITUATIONS IN THE HOODZ.

(Taken from the Hoodzville books collection)
larrywkeys@hotmail.com
Larrywkeys.com or HOODZVILLE BOOKS

Larry Keys
To Lisa: thanks For
Listening !!

42769058R00117

Made in the USA
Middletown, DE
21 April 2017